Artifact

KT BOWES

KT Bowes

ISBN: 978-1-99-115461-3

Acknowledgement

To my friends in Market Harborough in memory of the good times spent there. You know who you are and how much you blessed my journey.

Chapter One

She hadn't meant to steal. It wasn't a conscious decision or her usual way of operating. The opportunity presented itself and she made use of it in a cold and calculating way. It proved easy, making the overwhelming sense of guilt so much worse as Lara handled the stolen item in gloved fingers. They trusted her. She took advantage. "What have I done?" she murmured to the empty room.

Escaped tendrils of her dark hair pitched forward over her shoulder as she sat hunched at the wooden table. She felt rotten, inside and out. A hand strayed to her face with the full intention of rubbing her eyes and noticing the gloved hand, Lara prevented the action. She couldn't ruin the only pair of cotton gloves she brought back with her. They ended up in her suitcase by accident and she needed to keep them spotless to handle the artifacts. Lara's crime meant this object and its companion were now her responsibility and the fact weighed on her heart. "I hope I can keep you safe," she whispered to the precious items.

In films and novels, the hero would fling such things into a leather satchel and leap onto a train or off a bridge into fast flowing water. Nothing but naïve fancy. Mistreatment and contact with the open air would ruin the artifacts in seconds. Nobody bothered to research anymore. They just spat out a money-making film in which ancient maps were carelessly unrolled to deliver their secrets and then shoved back into a map carton without apparent damage. Lara's experience and years of training told her differently. Even the act of unrolling after so many years of storage would cause them to rip and crumble, not to mention the other terrible and yet exciting exploits the viewers watched them endure. Even the most robust parchment would become confetti before the end of the final credits.

Lara sighed and leaned back in the dining chair, the elderly wooden slats pressing against her spine. Exhaustion gnawed at her bones. She'd spent the arduous flight from New Zealand fraught with terror. Any of the customs checkpoints represented a threat to her stolen cargo, especially if someone already reported it missing. Sydney, Bangkok, Dubai, London. Lara retraced her journey of two years ago; only the return journey didn't contain excitement or anticipation. Her actions laced it with sleeplessness and misery.

To be caught transporting one item could have been down-played as accidental, but not two. She transported the brooch with frightening ease. Deciding to carry it in plain sight seemed the most logical disguise, and so Lara wore it on the front of her jumper, under her coat. She stole the items with surprising effortlessness. Covering her tracks seemed harder, but transporting the pin and manuscript was a complicated feat of ingenuity. The customs officer in Sydney noticed the brooch, catching sight of it as Lara leaned forward to stuff her passport back into the brown handbag slung across her body. "That's stunning," she gasped. "It must have cost you a fortune. Where did you get it?"

Lara smiled and brushed off the compliment. "It's just costume jewellery. I got it from one of the cheap shops in Auckland." Lara winced at her own lie, a complete betrayal of the priceless nature of the Māori *taonga*. Centuries old, it dripped with tribal history and *mana*. The customs officer nodded and shrugged and Lara worried for hours afterwards, waiting for the inevitable hand on her shoulder.

The manuscript was much harder to conceal. Lara couldn't allow it to venture into the hold of the mighty plane. Too much could go wrong. It might get stolen or damaged and rendered worthless. Lara kept it in her carry-on bag, sealed inside a double layer of plastic oven bags to keep it apart from the other objects in her rucksack. The cover of the book, made from ancient swamp kauri, weighed her down and put her hand luggage overweight. But the attendant at the check-in desk smiled and waved her through to her gate. It took Lara a while to calm down once on the plane. She sweated in terror, which left her skin cold and tacky afterwards, but the shakes took longer to subside.

Having survived three unique customs checks on her trek home, Lara most feared those at Heathrow. They were no more thorough than their equivalents overseas, but once on the home strait, Lara expected fate to take an upper hand in her escape. Sod's Law and the other helpful academics dictated it would all go hopelessly wrong at the last hurdle. It didn't.

As Lara approached the penultimate gate to freedom with her heart pounding and her head struggling to stay clear and rational, she found the desk vacant. Nobody waited at Heathrow arrivals' terminal to examine either her bags or her. Lara followed the signs for those with something to declare, her chest heaving and her gaze darting around her. She looked and felt like a criminal and waited for judgement. Someone *would* inspect her bags; that's what happened at airports. Her aunt insisted she bring back some New Zealand chocolate laced with native fruit. That at least needed to be checked. But the final desk before freedom proved empty.

Obeying the signage with a shaking hand, Lara lifted the wall phone and a chirpy voice asked her, "Do you have something to declare, Madam?"

Lara's brow furrowed as she named the chocolate and other food items Aunt Catharine demanded.

"Proceed to the exit, Madam, and welcome home," came the distant voice through the telephone. Game on.

It was cold, wet and much too late for someone who hadn't slept for just over thirty hours. Lara's strength flagged as she wrapped the beautiful pin inside a muslin bag and reunited it with the manuscript. Aunt Catharine had a safe stored underneath the stairs in an invisible cupboard and Lara locked the items in the bowels of its metal stomach and clicked the door shut. She replaced the secret panel and stood up, dismayed to find the sense of her heavy burden remained.

Alone in the three-storey house on Nithsdale Avenue, the silence of a Market Harborough October night embraced her. It folded her in as though she'd done nothing more exciting than put out the rubbish. The occasional hiss of passing car tyres in the rain outside reduced her sense of isolation as she contemplated people returning home to the warm welcome of family or friends. She heard the sounds of their safe, guiltless lives going on outside in the street. She resisted engaging with them by watching through the window. "It's better this way," she sighed.

Aunt Catharine had met her at the little train station in Market Harborough in her ancient Ford Fiesta. Lara permitted herself a tight smile at the comforting sight of the familiar red vehicle. "Oh, I know, I know," her aunt humphed. "Still hauling my sorry ass about town, poor old thing. But I'm hardly ever here, so there's no point owning something expensive to sit in the garage, is there?"

Lara refused to comment or pass judgement on the sound but tired looking vehicle. She knew how it felt.

"I've done some shopping," Catharine barked as Lara wheeled her suitcase towards the boot of the compact car. "You'll have to shove your luggage in the back seat."

Lara's case perched behind the driver, nodding with precarious imbalance every time she steered around a corner almost on two wheels. The boot turned out to be crammed with food from the local supermarket.

"It's all for you," Lara's aunt said as she slung the car into the garage at the back of the house. "I'm leaving in just under an hour. I thought you might be too tired to drive or shop and I'd got rid of everything ready to leave. Your phone call came as a surprise. Are you sure everything's all right?"

Lara nodded, not wanting to reveal anything to the woman she adored most in the world. Even one small chink in her armour might cause everything to come tumbling out, and she couldn't risk that. Catharine disgust terrified her, and it mattered what her aunt thought. It mattered even more what she might do about it.

As the taxi honked its horn in farewell and Lara closed the door behind her aunt's departure, Lara rested her head against the cold, painted wood and sighed. Catharine thanked her for looking after her elderly cat and sparing the need for him to go into a cattery. Lara smiled and tried not to dwell on the irony. She had nowhere else to go. As Lara unloaded the groceries, Catharine spun her busy way towards Manchester Airport and a six-month secondment in New York. Too late, Lara remembered the chocolate in her suitcase. A quick text to her aunt netted the response, *'It's for the neighbour. He'll be back on Monday.'*

Lara sat on the stairs with a sheet of handwritten instructions in her lap, allowing a sense of relief to work its magic on the chemicals in her brain. Marble, the elderly tabby cat, had a full A4 sheet of directions that she should follow. Lara sighed as the words jumped around on the page. The family treasures, or *taonga,* snuggled together in the safe just a few feet away and her chest tightened in silent misery. Attempting to break their hold on her psyche, she wandered around the house exploring, poking, and prodding things with feigned interest.

Catharine didn't go in much for pretentiousness and so Lara smiled to herself at a framed photograph of her aunt posing with Bill Gates. The photographer had snapped it at a glitzy celebration and she wore a long, shimmery silver dress. Her bright blue eyes, identical to Lara's, possessed an iridescent quality and Catharine beamed into the camera lens, which was a rare occurrence. Her aunt appeared clipped and professional, highly organised, motivated and, to the continued surprise of many, unmarried. She seemed to have discovered the secret to happiness and fulfilment alone, didn't suffer from loneliness or the lack of being part of a couple, and commanded a small entourage of devoted employees with admirable results.

"I should try it," Lara sighed with sarcasm, catching sight of her dishevelled self in the full-length mirror near the window.

Apart from the blue eyes, Aunt Catharine looked as different from Lara as a bicycle from a bus. Lara's genes commanded a delicate frame, but Catharine appeared solid and imposing. Lara's father's genes dictated darker skin for his daughter and the curly black hair everyone admired but wouldn't want to own permanently. But Aunt Catharine was Lara's lighthouse throughout most of her life, rescuing her when she needed it, as she did now.

With her habitual generosity, Catharine allocated Lara the enormous bedroom at the front of the house with the integral ensuite bathroom. Her aunt had owned the house for five years and knocked around the interior. The back of the floor resembled a hotel suite, with a large bedroom, walk-in wardrobe and ensuite. Catharine's clothes still covered the double bed. It appeared she'd packed in a rush. Lara itched to tidy up the mess, but left it for another day. Would Catharine expect to find everything as she left it, albeit covered in a six-month layer of dust? Or would she hate the idea of Lara putting her undies and bra away for her? "I'll deal with it tomorrow," she told the curious cat who peeked out from under her aunt's bed.

On the third floor was an attic bedroom, complete with its own ensuite. The abundance of ensuite almost made the family bathroom on the ground floor redundant, but the luxury of a large spa bath redeemed it. Tucked into the apex of the roof, the attic room gave the house its pointed appearance from the street. It disturbed the image of little sealed boxes sitting in a row for miles in either direction. Inside, the muted beige and brown decor gave the rooms a tasteful face. Lara had never visited this house. Catharine always travelled to see the struggling Lara, took her out for the day or invited her on holiday. It proved an unfamiliar experience to find herself on her aunt's home turf.

Lara climbed into bed, gratified by the cat's appearance. He pushed his scratchy way inside the bed covers with her. At least it wasn't so lonely with him there, especially as he had such a noisy purr. "Just don't die in the next six months," Lara whispered to him. "I'm in enough trouble as it is."

The old cat purred harder and dug his claws into her thigh as though trying to reassure her he possessed a substantial grip on life. Despite the pristine condition of the house, everything seemed small and old after the expansiveness of New Zealand. The roads were narrow and impossible to negotiate, and Lara's heart quickened at the thought of hurling the Fiesta around town. The house towered above the street, joined to others on either side in an interminable row of buildings in never ending perpendicular streets. Already the greyness of the cloudy skies into which her plane descended filled Lara with a sense of entrapment. She missed the giant blue New Zealand sky.

As she drifted off to sleep, muttering and twitching in her distress, Marble watched her through a chink in the covers with his one good eye. In her exhaustion, Lara misread the feeding instructions for the wily old moggy and one teaspoon of meat had translated into one tablespoon. He licked his paw and then stretched out against the newcomer and hoped she'd memorised the instructions, so she need never read them again.

Chapter Two

Lara slept for twelve hours straight, waking up just before midday. She lay still for a while, trying to ignore the increasing urge to visit the bathroom. Half an hour later, she dragged herself down to the long galley kitchen, nosing in the fridge for something quick to eat. Marble appeared through the cat flap and wound himself around Lara's legs, purring his affection for his alternative food source.

"Fine!" Her fraying nerves snapped. After he legged her up twice, Lara resorted to scraping the awful tinned meat into his bowl. "Stay there and eat that. But gulp it fast. It stinks."

She'd intended to keep him isolated in one spot, and it worked for as long as his furry face remained pushed into his food bowl. Then he occupied himself with a thorough wash, involving every tufty part of him. Lara poured herself a bowl of cereal, drowned it in milk and devoured it, satiating her starvation after her coma-like-sleep.

A knock on the front door a few hours later found her dressed and attempting to stuff her clothes into the drawers in her borrowed bedroom. The woman on the doorstep waited with patience as Lara hauled the door open and then grappled to retrieve the newspaper and envelopes which prevented its progress. Standing up too fast, Lara gasped as the world swam before her eyes. Her embarrassed pink cheeks faded to a sickly grey, and the visitor frowned in concern. "Sorry, sorry," Lara said, waving her free hand whilst her other one kept the myriad envelopes sealed in a death grip. "I stood up too fast. It's the jetlag. I forgot post came through the front door and not into a post box on the street."

The woman ventured into the hallway and took hold of Lara's arm. "Do you think you're going to faint?" she asked and Lara shook her head, determined not to make any more of an idiot of herself than she already had.

"I'm Kerry," the woman said. She offered her handshake despite the awkwardness of their proximity in the narrow hallway. "I live next door."

Lara smiled and prepared to offer her own name, but the guest waved her hand in dismissal. "Catharine asked me to check on you, just for the first few days, anyway. She thought you might like some help to find your way around Harborough. Said she felt disappointed that she wouldn't get to spend any time with you, but I don't mind showing you round when you're ready."

Lara liked her no-nonsense manner. With blonde hair folded into a messy bun, Kerry stood a head taller than Lara. Her open comportment gave her an instant appeal. Aged somewhere in her early thirties, Kerry dressed in a mixture of casual and formal attire. An unmistakable handprint in yellow paint marked the hem of her long grey skirt.

Lara closed the front door and her legs shook as she made her way along the hallway to the dining room and into the galley kitchen beyond it. Kerry slipped off her winter boots and followed, seeming at ease in the house.

She pulled out one of the dining chairs and slumped into it with a sigh. "Oh great!" she groaned, as the yellow handprint revealed itself when she crossed her legs. "I hate art."

Lara looked across at her in amusement as she flicked the switch to boil the kettle. She reached beneath the sink for a packet of cleaning wipes she'd found earlier when searching for the washing up liquid. As Aunt Catharine's old chintz teapot nestled on its trivet in the centre of the table to brew the tea, Lara rounded up cups, milk jug and sugar. Then she plonked her bottom into a seat opposite her guest.

Kerry continued to mop at the paint stain, while Lara fiddled around with the drinks. But the visitor studied the pretty brunette from beneath her eyelashes. "I thought you'd look like Catharine," she commented. She eyed Lara's long dark hair, which curled at will and framed her delicate face. Strands wriggled free and hung over her shoulders as though artfully arranged. "You're very tanned," Kerry continued. "I can tell you just left a New Zealand summer. Half your luck." She smiled at Lara and wrinkled her nose.

Dark lashes framed Lara's blue eyes, and she returned the smile. Her awkwardness and lack of confidence didn't fit with the image which Catherine painted of the globe-trotting archivist. "What day is it?" Lara asked, wincing at the strangeness of her question. "Sorry, jetlag. Again."

Kerry rose and dumped the cleaning wipe in the bin beneath the sink before answering. The handprint had morphed into a dirty yellow smudge around the bottom of her skirt. It appeared bigger, although a little faded. "Friday," she replied. "It's hard when you've crossed time zones, isn't it?"

Lara nodded and then remembered something. "Oh, Aunt Catharine asked me to fetch some chocolate and stuff from New Zealand for a neighbour. Is that you? I'll just nip upstairs and fetch it."

Kerry shook her head. "Not me. I'm allergic to dairy products. It might be the guy who lives on the other side of you. His accent might have a New Zealand twang. He's grumpy though, so I'd stay out of his way."

Oh great! Lara thought. *Now I have to take chocolate to a grumpy old man.*

Lara silenced, contemplating leaving the gifts for Catherine to deliver. It seemed unkind to leave them in the wardrobe for six months. She sighed, contemplating adding it to the various worries on her pile. They seemed myriad and plentiful.

"What were you doing in New Zealand?" Kerry asked. Lara rubbed her eyes, reluctant to speak about the last two years of wasted time. Kerry's expectant expression offered no opportunity for her to avoid the subject.

"I took a job cataloguing and restoring a collection of Māori artifacts for the most gorgeous old gentleman. He wanted to keep them for his family, to pass down the generations. It was a neat job, and I loved it."

"Was it temporary?" Kerry asked, pushing for more.

Lara nodded. "A year's contract at first, but then he extended it as we hadn't quite finished." Lara pressed her fingers into the corners of her eyes. She didn't want to think about Hone, about his gentle hazel eyes and gnarled olive hands, recounting the history of each object for her to record. His passion for his legacy had been pure and heartfelt. He loved his *whanau*, his family, and wanted his descendants to share in its rich tapestry. Lara hadn't realised she was crying until the hot wet tears sprinkled onto her face and then she felt mortified, dashing them from her cheeks and hoping no one saw them. Kerry pretended to examine the mess on her skirt, unsure what to do for the best.

Lara went into the kitchen for some kitchen roll and collected herself while she hunted in the pantry for biscuits. Then she came back to the table as though nothing had happened. "What do you do for a job?" she asked Kerry, keen to switch the attention away from herself.

"School teacher," she replied. "Hence the handprint. I teach the reception children down at the local primary school in Little Bowden. We can walk there one day if you like and I'll show you around."

Lara nodded, looking forward to the distraction of a walk. Her life stretched out in front of her. Six lonely months, as empty as the deserted house. "I thought all primary school teachers loved art and music," Lara commented with a smile. "Aren't they born with long print skirts and a guitar clutched to their breast?"

Kerry laughed, and for such an attractive woman, the hoot that emerged from deep in her stomach was a complete surprise. It was infectious and made Lara feel much lighter of heart. "Heck no!" she responded. "I loathe both activities. Unfortunately, they're the things the little darlings love best! I have a very competent classroom assistant who can play guitar and sing like an angel, so I only have to muddle through the art sessions at the moment."

"I loved art at school," Lara said, realising her error as Kerry's eyes shone.

"Done!" she cried, punching the air with her fist. "You can do next Monday's class. I'll bring the lesson plan round this weekend and we can go over it. I can't pay you though, does it matter?" She added the last sentence with a guilty wince, as though realising Lara might need to pay the electric bill or something. "I know! I'll pay you in dinners! You can eat at mine after work. Two dinners per class. What do you think?"

Lara's eyes bugged. '*Per class*,' sounded suspiciously like Kerry thought of it as a permanent arrangement. But Lara's six months appeared less daunting, and she capitulated with a regal smile, adding, "Well only until I get a job."

Kerry persuaded Lara to go out into the cold, dark evening and walk into town for chips. An English November was a shock to Lara's system after the balmy, sunlit evenings of a New Zealand summer. She wrapped herself up in a scarf and one of her aunt's overcoats and ventured into town with her new friend. She was very glad she had.

The little town was delightful. The grey concrete pavements and roads shone in the yellow glow of the streetlamps. Earlier rain added a glittery sheen over everything. The women strolled towards the end of Nithsdale Avenue and turned left onto the busy Northampton Road. Traffic had lessened in the hour since close of business and cars pulled up next to them at the traffic lights with Welland Park Road, exhaust fumes resembling yellow fog in the lights. Inside the vehicles, human beings resembled lumpy creatures, swathed in hats, scarves, snoods and thick coats. It seemed a far cry from the board shorts and flip-flops of a New Zealand summer.

Kerry pointed out the market hall across the road. "We can get the craft supplies from there tomorrow for the art class."

Lara cringed and tried not to dread it, distracted as Kerry entertained her with a story about a little girl who sat on the carpet during story-time and popped a coloured bead into her ear. "We called her mother, and she took her to the cottage hospital to have it removed. She regaled us for weeks afterwards with stories of a doctor wearing a head lamp and a pair of large tongs. For weeks afterwards, she drew these maniac pictures of doctors resembling strange insects with bug eyes and wings. We considered sending her to the educational psychologist."

Kerry's company was like a tonic for Lara, who seemed to have spent far too long feeling fraught and stressed, especially in the last few weeks. Her stay in Market Harborough had the vibe of a well-deserved break, although the need to secure paid employment still nagged at the back of her mind. The women purchased chips in a cone each, which Lara hadn't tasted for more than two years. She revelled in the decadence as they settled themselves on a bench in the centre of town. "They don't put vinegar on chips in New Zealand," Lara commented, her mouth packed full with the delicious, crunchy hot potatoes. "How can you not put vinegar on chips?"

Kerry nodded with encouragement. Vinegar ran down the side of a mouth stuffed to bursting. It sounded as though she said, "But all the salt will fall off."

Lara's eyes widened, and she made noises of complete agreement and then they sat in silence, enjoying both the food and their surroundings. Two man-made structures dominated the centre of Market Harborough. The first was St. Dionysius Church. "It dates back to 1300," Kerry told her. It appeared ornate in places, yet rugged and ancient in others. Darkness shrouded a sundial on the side, an addition from the 1700s. "During daylight hours,"

Kerry promised, "you can see an inscription. It says something about the time, I think. Someone added it in the mid-nineteenth century."

The structure possessed what Māori called *mana*, an inexplicable sense of power and influence. History held its roots and grounded it with the many who crossed its threshold over the centuries. Less than two hundred years gave New Zealand an enviable youthfulness. The wooden structures there fell victim to generations with no respect for history. They'd destroyed them with ease. But changing times meant they wanted everything back, longing for identity and desperate to make their mark on the world. The younger generation cast around for antiques to plug the historical gap and found them ruined or discarded. It was too late. Lara thought of the brooch and book in Catharine's safe and they drew her back to the smiling, wrinkled face of Hone. Sadness descended once again.

Kerry sensed the cloud of something almost physical shroud Lara and stopped her impromptu history lesson. "You ok, Lara?" She thought an archivist might be interested and confusion shrouded her.

"Yeah, just cold." Lara collected herself, not wanting her silence interpreted as rude. She conjured up polite questions about the building next to the church. "Is it the same era? It looks less old."

The Old Grammar School sat at the centre of a courtyard area, washed in a white glow from the floodlights built into the ground. A spectacular building built entirely from wood, it dated back to 1614, predating the English Civil War. As the headquarters for the King's army, Market Harborough housed his garrisons. The upper floor displayed classic Tudor features of white plaster with the familiar beams showing its age. A tiny window gabled into the slate roof revealed the attic level. "That's where the school teacher would have lived," Kerry told her. "Can you imagine me up there?"

Lara smiled, her gaze fixated on the ground floor of the building. It was the most astounding point of interest, because it didn't exist. Huge beam stilts buried in the cobbled ground allowed the area underneath the school to remain dry.

"They named the secondary school up the hill after Robert Smyth," Kerry informed her as she munched on her chips and avoided the scrumps of dairy-laden batter. "He went to London and made his fortune, kind of like Dick Whittington. He became Comptroller of the Lord Mayor's court in London and sent money back to build this original school here. It caused an outcry, because it was where the farmers sold their butter and other produce and so a compromise was to put the school up on stilts. Amazing architecture, isn't it, when you think what they'd have to go through to get it built without machinery?"

Lara nodded, feeling the steady, familiar curiosity burgeoning. She was desperate to see inside and it was comforting to know that despite recent events, her love of history was still intact. She stood up to put her chip wrapper in the dustbin and strolled around the building. Bible scriptures adorned the entire perimeter of the school, engraved into a beam which ran the entire length. Māori would respect the site as *tapu* or sacred. They used *rahui* to add spiritual integrity to an area of interest.

Hone possessed a *rahui* pole. *"Just as a symbol,"* he would say with a wink, but he would walk the boundary of his property, cradling it in his hand as he prayed divine protection over what his maker had allotted him. He inscribed it with his precise scripted hand in *Te Reo* Māori. The English translation was:

Psalm 91: 1-11 'Because you have made the Lord your dwelling place - the Most High, who is my refuge, no evil shall be allowed to befall you, no plague come near your tent. For He will command his angels concerning you to guard you in all your ways.'

Lara felt the tears close again and bit her lip to keep them at bay. She needed to get over this. How could she continue this new life if everything crowded in on her all the time? It was like trying to hold back a tsunami with her hand. Futile. She concentrated on breathing in through her nose and out through her mouth to regain control. By the time Kerry appeared next to her, having demolished her dinner and slung the wrapper in the bin, Lara had regained her composure.

Chapter Three

By Monday morning, the house to the left of Catharine's was still in darkness. Lights flicked on and off all weekend, but Lara assumed they were on a timer. The chocolate became quite floppy under the barrage from the central heating and she moved it to the fridge, where it adopted a ridged appearance under the wrapper. The word *pre-loved* sprang into her mind and Lara fought to get rid of it before it became any more embarrassing. She had asked Kerry in the pub on Friday night if the neighbour was away visiting grown-up children. Kerry hooted with laughter. "Grumpy git. I doubt it!"

Lara experienced anxiety about the art class and tried to cry off numerous times. Kerry remained dogged. "A deal is a deal. You're not ditching me now!"

It was agonising. Lara was still jetlagged and worry kept her up all night. The advent of 'Grandparents' Day' at the little primary school caused great consternation for all the teaching staff. "We're expected to teach our usual classes as well as create convincing, child-produced displays for the morning tea event. That's besides coercing busy parents into providing the cakes and goodies for the morning tea," Kerry complained. She joked Lara should attend the event, even though she wasn't a grandparent in any shape or form. "You'd enjoy it," she urged. She thought the children might get quite excited too but seemed to feel the steady flow of octogenarians would add more of a buzz than thirty-one rampant ankle biters.

In a last-ditch attempt to escape, Lara texted Kerry at midnight, informing her she had a headache and anyway, she didn't like children. Kerry astounded her by texting back straight away. *'That's ok. I don't like them either. See ya tomorrow.'*

Lara groaned. But she forced herself to dress and wait by the front door for Kerry's loud rap at eight o'clock on the dot. "I hate you already," Lara whinged and Kerry laughed it off as though the comment hadn't touched her at all.

They turned right at the end of Nithsdale Avenue this time, heading towards a figure in a bright yellow overcoat. Lara hadn't seen a lollipop lady in over two years and the sight stunned her. The woman resembled a fluorescent tube, even down to her hat and wellington boots. Lara looked at her lollipop, bearing the word 'Stop'. A silhouette of two children walked hand in hand as a warning to motorists. Lara imagined possessing the power to stop traffic, even if she needed to dress up like a beacon to do it.

It reminded her of her own childhood and filled her with happy sensations. When she dawdled to watch the bouncy lady perform her duties, Kerry grabbed her arm as though she were a child and hauled her to the central island. The lollipop lady ran behind and stopped traffic on the other side. "I forgot all about those," Lara commented and heard a giggle come from behind her. A group of like eight-year-old girls overtook the women, shouting a cheery,

"Good morning," at Kerry. Lara didn't realise for a minute they spoke to Kerry.

"What did they just call you?" Lara asked, catching her up as they passed down a narrow lane filled with tiny houses on both sides. Kerry answered her, but Lara had to ask again as she mumbled it.

"Mrs Christmas!" Kerry hissed. Lara's eyes widened in her olive face, looking like enormous blue marbles.

"Are you?" Lara whispered, and it was almost comical, the childlike awe in her expression. Kerry turned and marched on, making the smaller woman bounce along to keep up with her.

"Yes," she snapped. "Well, not the real one obviously, but yes, that's my name."

"Am I allowed to ask where... Mr..."

"No!" Kerry responded with a bite to her tone. "He might be in the North Pole for all I care. I divorced him and I'm not interested where he is." Lara felt sorry and looked contrite. Kerry's expression softened. "And before you ask why I didn't dump the awful surname and go back to my maiden name, it was Windass."

Despite trying very hard not to, Lara snorted and sniggered along the length of the pathway to the school. They passed through a beautiful green recreation ground, which Kerry hurried through at speed. She called over her shoulder, "This is Little Bowden Rec. The council own it and we play sports out here."

Lara dispensed with her giggles, provided she didn't think about a teacher with the surname Windass. She stopped herself considering the various permutations sought by naughty schoolchildren or out-of-work-archivists. As she dawdled under the canopy of ancient, giant oak trees, a falling stick whacked Lara on the head.

Disturbed by a sparrow busy doing last minute maintenance on his nest, it landed on the floor next to her boot. Kerry stopped by a high boundary wall and waited for her as Lara wandered up, shaking her head. "Serves you right!" she commented as Lara rubbed at a sore spot on her crown and looked backwards toward the offending tree.

"It was a stick," she said, ceasing her rubbing.

"Pity," Kerry retorted with a smirk. "I hoped it was sh... oh, hi Sharon."

A small girl with enough bunches in her hair to appear painful widened her eyes and parted her lips into a startled expression. Sharon's extensive ponytails covered her entire head. *Her mother must be an octopus,* Lara thought to herself. *Or get up every morning at five.*

"Morning Mrsss Chrissstmassss," the child shot over her shoulder in a cute sing-song voice with a lisp on the letter, 's.'

The snort of hilarity popped out before Lara had time to control it and she clapped her hand over her mouth. Kerry gave her a look of pure derision, following the little girl through a gate in the wall and up a high step into the playground. The child scrambled over the lip, holding onto the wall. Lara followed and wondered how on earth she could survive the next hour.

The forebears of Market Harborough created a school building with magnificent period features. It sent the historian in Lara into raptures. At over a hundred years old and steeped in memories, it captured her imagination. The original sections of the building had Victorian overtures. Red brick built with a sharp apex roof and the characteristic gable ends of the period it peeked over a high wall into the park. The windows were long and thin, rounded on the top without bowing to the severe arches of previous eras, individual panes of glass set into complicated wooden frames. It gave Lara a sense of security, creating a timeless solidity just by being there. It was a sensation she craved and the reason she was an archivist. She hunted for things to ground herself, historical facts and realities that gave her life a security it once had, but lost.

Inside, solid, dark wood floors revealed an oak grain. They shone with the love and care invested in their maintenance. Thousands of feet had passed over their surface, running, skipping, slouching, feet driven by childish elation or misery and bearing away future politicians, doctors, cleaners and astrologists. Each one as essential to somebody as the next set of small, twinkling toes.

Lara spent most of the morning in tears. Not out of sadness, but out of pure mirth and the sheer effort of keeping it under control. The room of four and five-year-olds proved they were both clueless and hilarious. In their little world, everything appeared catastrophic and every minor accident a tragedy. Lara didn't know how Kerry coped with it every day of her working life. Kerry allowed the art session to run into the next lesson with a glare at Lara. "We haven't finished our works of art," she declared, ignoring the fact that the archivist had a pounding headache and a bizarre urge for a large, unadulterated gin.

"You laugh a lot," one little boy commented to Lara, as she poured glitter on his horrific picture of his grandma. He spread creamy glue around his chin like shaving cream. Lara didn't know whether to take the comment as appraisal or criticism, but she bit her lip when she noticed him trying to shave with a plastic ruler. She couldn't ask for clarification because he'd glued his lips shut.

The poor classroom assistant seemed to spend her entire working life shepherding one or other of the children to the toilets to correct some misadventure. Lara hadn't seen her stand up straight yet and wasn't entirely sure if she could. Every time she saw the poor woman, her back was bent into a banana shape as she walked behind some three-foot-high human being. She reached forward, gripping a pair of dirty arms, and steered the owner of them down the corridor. Again.

Kerry introduced Lara to the children as a 'special' guest and also as an 'archivist'. That heralded two interesting problems. The first involved the unfortunate word, '*special*'.

"Are you special needs?" asked a little girl with long, flaming red hair and freckles. She had wedged two white glue spatulas into her ears, so they stuck out sideways from her head. It didn't matter what Lara answered as the child's, "What? What you sayin'?" punctuated everything she said. The little girl drew closer and closer to Lara's face to lip-read.

The noble classroom assistant took her to first aid and appeared without her. She'd glued with the wrong end and the secretary summoned her mother for another trip to the hospital.

"*Are* you special needs, then?" The speaker sat next to her at the miniscule table. He tipped sideways on his chair. Lara shook her head and avoided using the word again, realising its utterance attracted the attention of all the small people in the room.

A dreadful wailing noise began on the other side of the class and Lara cringed as Kerry tried to understand the problem. "Somebody's stolen grandma!" a small, brown-haired girl-child sobbed.

Kerry steered her over to Lara and shot her a triumphant look. Lara hadn't quite gotten over the urge to snort with laughter every time a child used the teacher's name. Kerry glared at her. "Lara will help you make a new grandma," she said, plonking the child into the seat on the other side of her and slapping a clean sheet of paper onto the table. Lara looked satisfyingly lost and Kerry flounced off to break up a dispute over a red crayon.

Half an hour later and the glittery grandma had lost the horror vibe. The shaver returned from the toilets with a very pink face and seemed thrilled with his sparkling family member. Lara had just about helped the girl with the 'lost' grandma to complete another. "What's an arch-iv-ist?" the shaver asked her. "Do you make arches then?"

Lara shook her head. "No, I deal with old things, make them better and keep them safe."

"Oh," piped up the child next to her. "Do you want my grandad? Mum's sick of him. We can drop him off at your house."

She looked so eager Lara wasn't sure how to answer without causing immense disappointment. "Well, I don't deal with living things," she responded, biting her lower lip.

The shaver's eyes bugged in his head, stark against his white, blonde hair. "Take mine then. She's died. That's why I maked her a zombie!"

Lara gulped as the little girl next to her stood. The tears had dried on her pretty freckled face and left strange white track marks in the smatterings of glue. "Mrs Christmas!" she yelled as though it was an emergency. "Look at mine."

As the hefty and indelicate snort escaped Lara's nose and mouth, she also noticed the 'lost grandma' attached to the back of the child's skirt. She had sat on her original work of art and no one had stolen it. An abomination of glitter and one stuck-on wobbly eye peered at Lara as the child sashayed across the room. Lara realised without preamble that she wasn't cut out for teaching and still didn't like children.

Chapter Four

Lara escaped from the school unscathed and even found her way home again without the help of the lollipop lady. At home, she opened a bottle of red wine Catharine left for her and plonked herself down in the lounge at the front of the house. She lay back in her armchair and pushed her slippered feet onto the ottoman, taking a well-deserved sip of wine and sensing the ache as her body relaxed.

The sound of the doorbell shrilling into the echoing hallway made her jump and wine slopped onto her sleeve. Lara swore and counted herself fortunate. Her drooping head indicated the fate of the wine could have been much worse, especially on Catharine's expensive cream sofa.

Lara stumbled to the front door, rubbing the sleep from her eyes. She peeped through the spy hole in the centre of the front door, squinting to make sense of the view. Her sleep befuddled mind experienced confusion at the darkness beyond the distorted glass. Lara shook her head and hissed, sure she'd slept for less than an hour. Her fingers fumbled for the outside light switch and she flicked it twice, surprised when it had no effect. When the doorbell rang again, she jumped and listed sideways. The irritating trill almost deafened her. She flung the door open and gaped into the street in surprise.

A tall man stood on the step. The dark blue of his suit jacket explained the confusing view through the spy hole.

Lara rubbed her eyes and then noticed the red stain on her white sleeve. She put her hand behind her back to hide it. The man on the doorstep appeared more than handsome and verged on striking. He possessed demarcated muscle tone that gave his expensive suit definition without the solidity of a weightlifter. Dark irises studied Lara, taking in her black hair and olive skin. The severe gaze offered no lightness or indication of friendship. "Why were you flashing the outside light?" he demanded. His baritone turned the question into a reprimand. "Is it some kind of distress call for alcoholics?"

Lara gaped. "I'm not an alcoholic!" she replied, an indignant whine entering her voice.

"Well, it's only just after twelve, you've spilled it on yourself and you look drunk."

Lara was both hurt and embarrassed. Not an impressive combination for making new friends. "What do you want?" she snapped, her tone aggressive.

The man inhaled, sensing himself on safer territory as she met his rudeness with her own. Perhaps masochism made him want everyone to treat him with disdain. "Key," he said. But that was all he said. No explanation. Just one word.

"Er, nope," Lara replied, her brows drawing into a line. "Still not understanding you." Without stopping to consider her options, she slammed the front door in his face. She retrieved the glass of wine from the lounge and put it on the side in the kitchen. Then she went upstairs and changed her shirt, taking time to run the stained one under the sink in her ensuite, delighted when it came out with soap and a lot of rubbing.

The sight of the letterbox opening and a pair of dark eyes peering through the gap, alarmed Lara as she walked downstairs with a pile of washing. "Catharine had my key," came a disjointed voice. "I need it back. I can't get in next door."

Tired, fed up and not best pleased at finding herself humiliated by a tall, dark stranger, Lara slammed the kitchen door on him as well. She managed not to drop her bundle of washing, which would have furthered her embarrassment as it contained her underwear. She loaded the washing machine, sipped her wine and made a sandwich for lunch. The sound of meowing came from the other side of the back door and without thinking, Lara opened it, wondering why Marble hadn't used the cat flap at the bottom. The stranger stood on the back doorstep, holding the cat at arm's length so as not to get fur on his suit.

He put the cat down as soon as Lara closed her astounded mouth. "Can we start again?" he asked, but there was still an edge of sarcasm in his tone. Lara stared at him hard and tried to dispel the urge to shout, 'No!' and slam the door in his face again. Instead, she asked him how he got into the back garden.

"I took a long walk round to the street behind and let myself in the back gate. You should keep that locked for your own safety. I've locked it now. After a twelve-hour flight, I'm tired and my suitcase is still on my front doorstep for anyone to steal. I'd appreciate my key now. *Please.*"

Lara stood back with reluctance to let him step over the threshold. His hair had a windswept appearance and tiredness shrouded him. It might account for his characteristic grumpiness. “The thing is,” Lara started, “I’m just house sitting for my aunt. I don’t know where your key is. She just asked me to give you some chocolate. And I’m not an alcoholic. I just spent the morning helping a friend and my body still thinks it’s ten o’clock on Friday night after my *twenty-four*-hour flight, so I know how tired looks.”

The man sighed, a breath which escaped with exaggerated force. He moved past Lara, heading for a cupboard over the washing machine. He reached in and took a wine glass, pouring himself a decent slug from Lara’s opened bottle. *How come everyone in the street seemed to know their way around Aunt Catharine’s home?* Perhaps she held dinner parties and had tried to get Kerry and this man together. It was just the thing she *would* do. “Aunt Catharine’s in New York,” Lara replied. “I can try to text her.”

The man tutted and took another drag of the wine. “I know where she is!” he retorted, his tone rough. He ignored her while he took a phone call on his mobile, swigging a second glass of her special wine at the kitchen table. “Arama!” he snapped. Finishing the call after a few grunts, he turned to face Lara. “Catherine said she left a sheet of instructions.”

Lara’s face lit up as she digested this latest piece of news, particularly the part about the sheet of instructions. “Now, where I she put it?” With great difficulty, she cast her mind back to Friday night and did a curious retracing of her steps, which the exasperated traveller sat down at the table to observe. With an exclamation of success, Lara drew its folds from the dresser drawer in the hallway and spread it out. “Oh crap!” she muttered upon reading it.

The stranger ran his hands across his eyes and took another swig of the wine. "What?" he asked. His tone held a guarded vibe, as though he didn't want the answer.

"It's ok," Lara replied, poking around on one of the top shelves of the dresser. "Your key is in an envelope...here!" She drew it out in victory and then glanced at Marble with concern. "But I've been overfeeding the cat."

The man left with his key and Lara heard him dragging his suitcase over the doorstep and into his hallway. Their front doors were centimetres apart and the houses, mirror images of each other. It meant Lara also heard him fall up the stairs and swear. She smiled to herself as she pictured the image of him flat on his face. *How on earth does lovely Aunt Catharine put up with him next door?* She wondered. But then perhaps it explained why, as he arrived home, Catharine left. Even she wanted to avoid him.

Lara cleared away Arama's glass and her own and switched the washing from the machine to the dryer in the laundry room at the very end of the house. She opened the window and stuck the dryer hose out of it to encourage the condensation to leave the building and set it going. Then she went to sit down in the lounge and watch some daytime television and woke up four hours later.

Chapter Five

"You will not believe this!" Kerry's eyes bulged with excitement. "Do you remember the cute little girl with the auburn hair and freckles?"

Lara tried not to shudder at the memory of the art lesson from hell. It was over twenty-four hours ago, but the lasting effects seemed permanent. Lara nodded with feigned politeness.

"Well," Kerry began, "she went home and told her mother you were an archivist and she came to see me..."

"The little girl came to see you?" Lara asked confused and Kerry bridled, annoyed at the derailing of her story.

"No! Her mother. She's in charge of the museum in town and she's been looking for someone to sort out some of their collections. She's persuaded the council to stump up some money on a part time basis and she wants you to ring her tonight. I told her you help me on a Monday morning and she agreed that was fine. They can work around that, seeing as it's so important to you...me...well, both of us." Kerry finished with a flourish. Lara kept her eyes glued to the pink and yellow blob-remains of a fruit salad chewy sweet in the front of Kerry's blonde fringe. She wondered if it was hers or someone else's.

The prospect of regular hours daunted Lara, but Kerry's offer of visiting Hades every Monday for the next six months terrified her. She considered texting Aunt Catharine, apologising for letting her down and leaving Market Harborough. To go where though? How many more fresh starts did one person need?

"Ring her then!" Kerry pressed, shoving a scrappy piece of paper with a phone number on it towards Lara.

Half an hour later and Lara had secured three days' work a week, down at the local museum in Harborough. Despite her ditzy appearance, the little auburn-haired girl-child proved succinct in her recount of Monday's art lesson. Her mother had manoeuvred and schemed since hearing her tale. She sounded capable on the telephone and Lara felt the familiar excitement bubble in her chest as she thought about cataloguing systems and repair work to artifacts and manuscripts. Her heart constricted as she passed the bottom of the stairs on her way to the lounge to tell Kerry the splendid news. Hone's possessions seemed to cry out to her from their hiding place.

Lara didn't seem as enthusiastic as Kerry anticipated. She seemed reserved and the lingering sadness took a grip on her again. In truth, Lara sat opposite her new friend and wondered if Kerry would like her as much if she knew what she'd done.

Later on, tucked up warm in bed, Lara lay listening to the sounds coming from next door. The headboard of her double bed touched the adjoining wall and when she reached her hand back, she felt the vibrations from a wall-mounted television in the bedroom next to hers. His name *was* Arama. Kerry laughed at the tale of their first meeting and confessed she avoided him. "What a shame," Lara commented. "You could have ditched your surname in favour of his. I'm sure Aunt Catharine would be happy to rig it all up for you."

Kerry scoffed. "No, thanks! I think I'll stick with what I have rather than take his weird surnames."

"Weird?" Lara cocked her head.

"Yeah, he has two. One is English and the other has a heavy accent. I think he's from Australia or New Zealand."

Lara gulped and bit the inside of her lip to keep control as something massive clicked in her head. *Of course, you stupid woman*, she chided herself, recalling Arama's dark hair and features and his long, regal nose. He possessed the genetics of a Māori chief depicted in the sepia photographs. It also explained the New Zealand chocolate Catharine made her bring home. Lara knew with certainty she needed to stay away from him.

The joke in New Zealand was that only two degrees separated everyone. They were all related by birth or marriage to each other. If Lara proved very fortunate, it would be a while before anyone missed the artifacts she'd stolen. But a chance conversation with Arama might track back to someone in New Zealand and conclude her attempt to hide her theft. Added to that, her own conscience troubled her daily and she couldn't risk it. "Stay away from the man next door," she whispered to herself in the darkness. "It shouldn't be too hard. He's horrible."

Lara turned over in bed and groaned at the thought of the chocolate downstairs in the fridge. She resolved to write a brief note and shove it through his front door before work the next day.

That would have to do.

Chapter Six

"You're in a real skills-shortage area. You have no idea how hard it's been to find someone to take care of this," Angela Macdonald intoned with a smile of gratitude. "Oh, we've got lots of inexperienced people, but no one who knows what they're doing. And it's so easy to make a terrible mistake and then something gets damaged and future generations just hate you for it." She looked just like her pretty daughter, with an unruly mop of bright red hair and a dusting of freckles. She possessed the same inquisitive expression.

"How's your daughter?" Lara asked. She cleared her throat and considered her words with care. "Did they remove the spatulas?"

The mother chortled with a good natured grin. "Kid's, hey. Who'd have 'em?"

Not me, Lara thought, but instead she replied, "I'm impressed your daughter knew what an archivist did. I didn't think she heard anything I said on account of the spatulas."

"Oh, she's a bright cookie," Angela smiled. "She doesn't miss much!"

The Harborough Museum was situated at the back of the Council Offices on Adam and Eve Street, in an impressive four storey brick building that was once a corset factory. It occupied part of a floor of the vast building, redesigned for functionality. A small shop and reception area nestled near the entrance alongside rooms for temporary or visiting exhibitions. Two main areas towards the back of the floor hosted an industrial display, and a town and village exhibition.

By far the most impressive collection was the Hallaton Treasure, which occupied a large area at the centre of the museum floor. It contained many coins found quite by chance near the village of Hallaton, proving to be one of the most prestigious finds in Britain and containing the oldest Roman coin ever discovered. The Iron Age site dated back to 50 AD and as well as over five thousand gold and silver coins, yielded clothing, jewellery, part of a Roman helmet, everyday items and animal bones.

Lara found the whole thing fascinating. She wandered around the museum looking into the glass cabinets and trying all the interactive tools and games designed to encourage children. It seemed unlikely Lara's collection would ever experience the stress of a public display. It was far too precious. Lara's work area consisted of a dark, windowless room at the back of the building. It would sound appalling to anyone else but it suited her for the purposes of dealing with the artifacts. Daylight could not gain access, for fear of it touching the manuscripts with its destructive smile.

Lara donned the familiar cotton gloves and set about examining the treasures. A builder working on a mysterious wiring problem in the interior of St. Dionysius Church uncovered a hidden entrance to a tunnel. After much deliberation, archaeologists exposed the orifice, brick by painful brick. They'd uncovered a priest hole, a tiny entrance to a tunnel leading up to the safety of the church spire. The town's ancestors had created an alcove between the walls, large enough for one or two people to hide. During dangerous stages of history, the ordained priests fled their attackers, concealing themselves in tiny holes, passageways, between walls and wherever they could. When Church and State clashed, many lost their lives as collateral damage.

Often the escape routes were hidden with such skill, they remained undetected for centuries. Building work exposed most priest holes, and many ended up bricked over or encompassed within a rebuild. The priests had gained access to the hole at St. Di's through the side of a pillar in the nave. The priests crawled upwards, using hand-holds to haul themselves through the vertical climb. They would have remained inside the tunnel until the soldiers left, which could have been days or weeks.

The genuine surprise came years later, from a person small and brave enough to crawl up the tunnel and reach the top. Inside on a high ledge, they discovered small animal bones with the likeness of chicken. Next to the remnants of the priest's meal, they found a set of dusty and decaying manuscripts, bound in leather and hand stitched. Lara's job was to inspect, stabilise and copy the manuscripts in digital and reproductive formats. She needed to interact with local historians and investigate any notable information found in the manuscripts. The difficulty was in maintaining secrecy. Nobody could know about the manuscripts. Not yet.

By the end of the first day, Lara had worked through every break. She left the room only to use the bathroom. Instead of leaving at four, the caretaker threw her out of the building when he locked up at five. Angela smiled and patted her on the shoulder as they met on the front steps.

"You've achieved a lot in your career," she said in passing. She fought with the catch of her umbrella before giving up and letting it fall to her side. "I've looked over your CV this afternoon."

Lara gave a polite nod and her lips tightened. She hoped Angela didn't notice how she tensed.

"Five years at the Tate Gallery is quite an achievement. And two years in New Zealand." She frowned. "The curator of the Tate sounded pleased you'd arrived back in the country. He asked me to pass on his regards and mentioned he'd love to hear from you." She raised a manicured eyebrow. "I hope you won't let him poach you from us."

"No." Lara swallowed and shook her head.

"I left an email message for your New Zealand referee. With a time difference of thirteen hours, I might have a reply by morning. It's all academic, anyway. A paper exercise. You're an absolute find. The board will understand that."

Lara nodded and walked home through the darkness experiencing more peace than she had for months. She left the upstairs lights on a timer and the front bedroom looked cheerful, casting a happy yellow glow onto the street. As she clicked the front gate shut behind her, Kerry's door whipped open and she called to Lara, "That's great timing. Dinner's ready if you're hungry?"

Lara wasn't sure she was. But then the unmistakable scent of shepherd's pie wafted down the street and her stomach gave an unhealthy growl. "Thank you so much, Kerry," she called back with gratitude. "I'm just going to feed Marble and then I'll be straight round."

She was as good as her word. Marble looked at her in disgust as the single loaded teaspoon of cat meat went into his biscuits. "Oh, stop it!" Lara chided him. "You couldn't have thought you'd get away with it for six whole months." She stayed at home only long enough to swish the bedroom curtains shut and change into track pants and a comfy sweatshirt. Then grabbing her mobile phone, Lara spun out of the front door and onto the path.

But she didn't look and ran straight into someone, winding herself and causing them almost to pitch over the low side wall. Lara's lungs locked, able to accept oxygen but not expel any. As she bent double, gripping her chest, she imagined her lungs exploding. She glimpsed a pair of trainers in her peripheral vision and realised the other person had been running past her. In her haste, Lara saw them too late. She felt as though she'd smashed into an immovable object, although she experienced gratitude for the muscular arms that prevented her from flying into the road and the path of a passing vehicle.

Her life flashed before her eyes in a series of white and black dots in her vision. As tears and snot dripped onto the pavement beneath her, she heard her chest make the most dreadful wheezing noises. She found herself apologising inside her own head for her myriad wrongdoings. *Sorry God, sorry God, sorry...* Nobody would know Hone's treasures nestled inside the safe and even when Catharine found them, she wouldn't know where they belonged.

Someone rubbed Lara's back and supported her around her waist. The air moved again inside her lungs by degrees. Great big wracking sobs shuddered out of Lara's delicate frame, huge enough to rock her body. At one point she battled the urge to vomit, but the sensation passed as her equilibrium returned. Her right side blossomed with unbearable pain when she tried to move. She reached her hand up to touch it with extreme care. Pain rocketed through her ribs, sending panic signals to her brain and Lara heard herself sniffing and crying.

Feeling the overwhelming urge to crouch down on the ground and take the pressure off her ribs, Lara clung to the strong arms that allowed her to sink but prevented her from overbalancing. Bending her knees and taking the weight of her body along her thighs, Lara used her left arm to brace herself on Kerry's front fence. She felt the sharp thorns of a rose bush cut into the soft pads of her fingers but at that moment, didn't care. It was the least of her problems.

Kerry's worried face appeared at the front door. Seeing Lara's prone shape on the ground and somebody stood over her, she panicked and sprang to her friend's defence. "Get off her!" she shouted, rushing forward in her slippers and negotiating the creaky front gate in one swift movement. To her dismay, Lara heard Arama's dulcet tones and cringed. She'd planned to avoid him, realising she'd forgotten to deliver the chocolate before work.

"Just shut up a minute." His voice held an unfamiliar alarm. "Help me get her inside, will you?"

Kerry tried to haul Lara up by her arm and she let out a groan that came from deep in her boots somewhere. Kerry made her second mistake of the night by releasing it, which only hurt even more. It brought further noises of misery from Lara and Kerry panicked. "What can I do to help?" she begged. "Tell me what to do."

Lara felt strong arms slide beneath the backs of her knees and around the left side of her waist as Arama lifted her.

It was a relief not to have to trust her own wobbly legs, and he carried her up the front steps and into Kerry's house. He laid her on the sofa in the front room and stood back to inspect her sorry state. "She needs to go to hospital," he concluded, observing her clammy white skin and sweat beaded on her forehead. Lara knew she needed to get it together, to avoid losing her new job after only the first day.

"No," she gasped. "I just need some tissues, please." Leakage from her eyes and nose ran down her cheeks and chin, sticky beneath her fingers. As Kerry dashed from the room on her mission, Arama squatted down next to the sofa, his face filled with concern.

"I'm so sorry," he whispered, and he looked and sounded genuine. Lara just felt embarrassed.

"I accept all the blame," she replied, "I didn't look before I dashed onto the street." She shook her head, annoyed at herself. Arama's brow knitted, and he used his right hand to brush Lara's dark hair off her face. A white tee shirt and running shorts made for an unusual winter ensemble. He left his trainers on in Kerry's lounge in his haste. She still hadn't returned with any tissues and Lara tried to use her hand to wipe the wetness from her face. To her surprise, Arama lifted the bottom of his tee shirt and used it to smooth away the tears and snot.

The tender, caring action presented a complete paradox to the man who drank her wine and demanded his key.

Lara concentrated on breathing and tried to get it together for everyone's benefit. When Kerry returned, she carried a whole toilet roll and broke off great swathes of it for Lara to blow her nose into. Her appetite abandoned her. Kerry laid into Arama for his carelessness and to Lara's surprise, he *didn't* blame the whole thing on her. As the pain medication numbed her lips, she decided she wanted her bed more than anything. "I'm sure I can sleep the pain off," she declared in a garbled mumble, wishing the desire into existence.

Despite the objections of her companions, she insisted on walking home, declining their offers of help with as much gratitude as she could muster. She dragged herself up the stairs, pausing after every second step. She slept in fitful bursts after her head hit the pillow, causing herself untold agonies every time she turned onto her right side.

Her dreams called up images of the manuscripts which she already knew by touch, illuminating the old English scribing inside them. The words of the sixteenth century priest came to her in her painful slumber, recounting his own nightmare existence of hiding in the walls of the church. Wonder filled Lara's chest when she held the delicate pages in her gloved hands, able to read those first lines. For what she held were the private records of the priests of St. Dionysius Church. In 1534, Henry VIII declared himself the spiritual head of the English Church through the Act of Supremacy and began dissolving the Catholic monasteries and appropriating their property and wealth. Priests needed to sign the Oath of Supremacy, swearing allegiance to him as Supreme Governor of the Church of England, instead of the Pope. For those who did not wish to conform, there was certain death as punishment for treason.

In 1553, with the accession of the Catholic Queen Mary, her religious views again threw the nation into chaos as she repealed the Act and persecuted Protestants. The manuscripts began around that time but were undated and anonymous. In her feverish sleep, the words of the priest ran through her mind like a cool waterfall.

'T'is but a short time since the King's men hunted us, forcing us to sign the infamous Oath or die. Now we have a different heir and she reviles the reformed church and spits on her father's grave. Now we must renounce it.

I wonder if there will come a time when the clerics of this nation are all gone, forced from their hiding places and made kindling for their fire. We pitch and toss, this way and that at the whim of our rulers, never knowing which way to run, only that our calling is to speak the Word of God. What hope is there for this world, if Satan's fires are permitted to burn relentlessly, unchecked by Heaven's army? We cannot fight this alone. Alas, it is not myself for whom I fear, but this sorry world which would seek to destroy that which does not please it or serve its purposes. This someday godless world will implode upon itself at the end of time, when Jehovah Jireh removes his hand.'

"I am godless," Lara's addled brain condemned her. "I am not worthy to read their words or touch their relics." Sobs of anguish and pain punctuated her speech and the dark silence of the night rebuked her further.

When morning came, Lara found it almost impossible to sit up in bed. It took her valuable minutes to work out how to roll onto her left side and then push herself upright. Any movement of her right arm caused a burning agony in her ribs. When she finally cleaned her teeth in the ensuite, she vomited blood, which both frightened and disgusted her. The face that peered back from the mirror appeared drawn and haggard. She showered and dressed as slowly as she dared. It proved a tedious and painful journey into work for her second day, taking double the time as she tried not to jolt her aching body.

Chapter Seven

The day dragged with an endless torture and Lara proved fragile, reluctant to venture even to the bathrooms downstairs. She wore cotton gloves, an apron and a facemask to protect the manuscripts as she performed her delicate work on them. The media reported the existence of the priest hole, but the books remained a well-kept secret. Once she'd stabilised and copied them, there might be something to show the world. They would only ever see the copies.

Lara used a fine brush and archival powder to dust the delicate pages of the manuscripts; each page dealt with painstaking care. The covers were filthy, sealed inside four centuries worth of dust and debris. Partially protected by a sackcloth bag, they'd remained hidden from the first visitors to the hiding place. But still open to the elements, they suffered damage. The manuscripts consisting of calf skin spent the first months of their life soaked in lime and alum to remove hair and any residual flesh, before being stretched on a frame. With their surface scraped down to a thin paper using a curved lunellum tool, they were dried and cut into sheets. Each sheet folded in half, created two folios, recto and verso. Smoothing with pumice helped the ink adhere. Lara stroked the delicate pages with care and respect as she cleaned them.

A robust manufacturing process produced quality and had assisted their survival. Margins pricked with an awl and lines ruled between them, betrayed their intention for use as something much more official. Lara wondered what induced the priest to take such an expensive item made with such painstaking precision - and use it as a diary. She imagined the stress of his split decision, made by a man who already certain of his death. Perhaps he had a long-sighted view, in which his memories might one day lead to the celebration of his tumultuous life. It seemed a pity his name remained absent from the old-fashioned script, blinding posterity to his existence. The church records might reveal his identity later with clever detective work.

Despite the direness of his circumstances, wedged into a space less than a metre wide and two metres across, the priest managed a legible hand. Tiny spots of candle wax dotted the pages in places, made brittle over time and giving no doubt as to the location of the missive's conception. The priest had compiled it inside the priest hole.

Scribed with a goose or swan feather, the strokes looked uniform and even. A penknife would have been used to erase any errors, scraping at the skin with care to remove the mistake. There was not much evidence of this, apart from a few deeper pock marks in the fabric, perhaps betraying someone in a hurry. The manufacturer created the ink from oak gall, thickened with acacia tree sap. Lara wondered how the priest transported it into the spire. After completing the first of the manuscripts, the maker inserted the folios inside one another to make a quire, before sewing them together. Lara had handled documents fixed between wooden boards, but these manuscripts involved delicate stitching. Nothing protected the first and last pages.

Lara wondered if the sewing process happened in the hiding place by the light of the candle, but she doubted it. Perhaps the sewing happened after the queen entered her grave, the manuscripts removed from the spire and bound. She worried her secret work with the manuscripts might increase the damage. Angela resisted engaging a forensics expert able to deal with such precious objects. Lara worried she might not persuade them to betray all of their secrets to her.

"We just can't afford it," Angela concluded. She watched over Lara's shoulder as she worked.

Lara winced. "But I don't understand why these manuscripts lack their leather covers. Where are the metal bosses or corners? I'm wondering if the stitching process took place in the spire." She shivered as she thought of it, glad she wouldn't need to make the climb herself to inspect the man's sixteenth century prison.

"It's possible." Angela twisted her lips. "But we have no more money to throw at this. Just do what you can for now."

Lara dated the four manuscripts by the events contained in their cursive text. From those first entries concerning Queen Mary's persecution of the protestants, it seemed the manuscripts had remained in the spire, added to by successive generations of priests. It made fascinating reading. It was a diary of the hunted.

There was an art to reading the written text and the untrained eye would have grown disinterested within a brief time. But mediaeval English was one of Lara's favourite subjects in university, taught to her by a formidable Welshman with a passion for his subject and numerous publications to his redoubtable name. It was just a matter of remembering the meaning of certain words, no longer in usage and understanding the different sounds created by symbols which appeared unbidden in the middle of indiscernible words. "What do you want to tell me?" Lara whispered to the fragile pages, hoping she could do them justice.

That day and the next passed with Lara engrossed in her work. True, she felt unwell and needed to keep still, but the manuscripts proved so fragile that sudden movements hindered her work, anyway. But by late on Friday, a dreadful pounding had begun in her head and her breathing sounded laboured and painful.

Making one of her routine visits to see Lara, Angela gasped with shock at her ghastly pallor and the sweat beading on her brow. She ordered Lara home and drove her there herself. "I promise I'll see the doctor if I need to," Lara assured her. The double yellow lines outside made it impossible for Angela to come into the house. She left, against her better judgement, trusting Lara to call the doctor as she'd promised. But once Angela drove away, Lara sank down on the stairs and leaned her head against the smooth balustrades.

Lara couldn't make it up the stairs to bed. She felt wretched. Marble came and wound himself around her legs but trying to stroke him jolted her body and increased the nausea. It was getting harder and harder to breathe and with a thudding realisation, Lara knew she needed the medical help Angela had offered. Somehow she crawled to the telephone and managed to fumble it into her hand. Aunt Catharine kept a business card for a taxi firm propped on the hall dresser and from the floor, Lara read the number and dialled it into the phone. Recognising the address, a cheerful dispatcher told her someone would be there within the next ten minutes.

It took five. The driver hammered on the door, forced to park illegally on the double yellow lines. Lara crawled to the front door on her hands and knees. She clawed her way up the wall and pull it open wide. White and clammy, she bent double in the doorway as the taxi driver eyed her with suspicion. "You won't throw up in my taxi, will ya?" he asked and Lara shook her head.

"Hospital," she said and when he looked at her in confusion, repeated it.

"Lara?" Kerry's concerned face appeared at the driver's shoulder and seeing her friend's terrible complexion, ordered him in her best teacher voice, "Help me get her into the car. Quick!"

The Accident and Emergency department of Kettering hospital was bleak. Not so much in the decor but in the waiting time, which was four hours. Lara sighed and postured, but Kerry forced her to sit in one of the metal framed chairs and wait for her, while she gave the receptionist her friend's details. When she came to sit back down, Lara's complexion turned from grey to white. Sweat dried on her forehead to leave smears in her makeup. Kerry rested her hand over Lara's clenched fingers, frowning at the tears which sprang into her eyes. "So how do we kill four hours then?" Kerry asked, once she'd read all the posters, leaflets and other paraphernalia available. Lara spent the entire time leaning back to take the pressure away from her ribcage. She propped herself in the uncomfortable seat with her eyes closed.

"I spy?" Lara suggested with sarcasm, but Kerry seemed to consider it as a serious proposal and rejected it.

"No, you need to keep your eyes open for that."

Lara breathed out, regretting the pain it caused. "I don't need this right now," she hissed. "Just as my life is going right for a change, wham! Literally. Oh, why did I not just look before I ran out of that stupid gate?"

Kerry settled into her chair next to Lara and turned sideways to stare at her friend. "Was your life that bad before now?"

Lara bit her bottom lip, knowing she'd said too much. She froze, keeping still and quiet. But Kerry's teaching experience equipped her with all the Pit Bull radar equipment designed to sniff out weakness, bullying, fake tears and all the other apparently 'innocent' wiles of small children. Including lies. She wasn't about to let it go. "Come on, Lara," she sighed. "I told you about Mr Christmas. The least you can do is level with me."

Lara made awful groaning noises to prevent herself from laughing. It proved a terrible idea alongside the thudding pain radiating from her side. The receptionist half stood in her seat as other patients turned to stare in Lara's direction. The woman behind the desk picked up her phone and made a call as a child with his head stuck in a casserole dish asked his mother with a peculiar echo, "What's that noise?"

"Ok then," Kerry pressed. "Tell me about your childhood. Catherine spoke about you a lot and how you'd gone to New Zealand, but apart from that, I only know she's your mother's sister."

"Was," Lara said with a frown. Her hand fluttered over her eyes. "She *was* my mother's sister."

"Oh," Kerry breathed. She winced with a flash of guilt. "I'm sorry; I had no idea."

"It's ok. Mum died a long time ago. I wish she were here now though. There are so many things I need to talk to her about..." Lara tried to sit forward and felt Kerry's supportive hand against her spine, the rubbing action reminiscent of something she might do to a five-year-old with an emotional problem. It proved comforting and tempted Lara to confide in her for real. Up to a point, that was. "I was ten when she died. She walked to school to meet me as a surprise. Mum worked as a secretary in a law firm and got off work early that day. Something distracted her half way across a busy road - nobody will ever know what. A vehicle hit her from behind and she died the next day. Dad found two cinema tickets in her handbag. She wanted to take me to see a chick flick for my birthday. Dad was away in Scotland on business and promised to be back for my actual birthday the next day. We were going to have a party. Instead, we sat together and held her hand while she died at tea time on my birthday. He never got over it."

"That's awful," Kerry breathed, her face a mask of misery. The mother with the casserole-dish-wearer wiped her eyes with a tissue.

"That's why Aunt Catharine's so important to me. She's been a real constant all the way through."

Kerry nodded in silent appreciation of her middle-aged neighbour. "I miss her when she's not here," she admitted. Catherine ran her IT firm with precision and professionalism. But during her messy divorce, Kerry had cried on her shoulder and drunk Catharine's wine on more than one occasion. "Tell me about your dad," Kerry suggested, hoping to lighten the mood a little. It seemed clear from other comments Lara made how much she adored her father.

"He died two-and-a-half years ago," Lara replied. Her eyes remained shut tight with pain, sparing her the view of an entire row of women opposite sharing tissues and hugs at her sad tale. One had her arm in a makeshift sling, one sported a chisel through her palm from trying to open a pot of paint, and the other accompanied her son who wore her favourite casserole dish. The small boy grew bored with the wait and attempted to dislodge his own head. The steady *thunk, thunk, thunk* of glass on lino punctuated Lara's story. "He got Leukaemia. We shared a house in London for a while until he went into the hospice. He told me about my Māori heritage. That's why I went to New Zealand after he died. The opportunity came out of nowhere and I just took it. Aunt Catharine paid for my flight and off I went. I look back now and I took such a risk. But it felt like home and I loved it." Lara turned towards Kerry, a note of urgency in her voice, "Please don't tell Arama about my heritage. I don't want him to know."

"But why did you come back?" Kerry asked and the women on the row opposite leaned forward as one.

Lara floundered. Without meaning to, she arrived back at the exact point she hadn't intended. She didn't want to go into it. *Please God, help me,* she pleaded in her head. *I know I don't deserve it but...*

"Oh, that was quick!" Kerry exclaimed as the Triage nurse called Lara's name. The small audience of women as one, looked devastated. It was like getting to the end of a gripping novel and discovering the back page missing. Annoyance turned to anger, and they glared at the receptionist as though it was her fault.

"Don't you dare break that!" the casserole dish owner shrieked, noticing her son thudding his fist against her best dish. “I need it later on for the spuds.”

Kerry helped Lara out of her seat and over to the nurse. They settled her into a cubicle and she sank onto the bed.

“The receptionist put you at the top of the list.” The nurse smiled. “She said you couldn’t breathe very well. Can you tell me what happened?”

Lara opened her mouth to speak at the same moment as the cough rose unbidden in her chest. With a groan of anticipated agony, she cupped her hand over her mouth to suppress the agony. The cough came anyway, bringing with it a small jet of blood and Lara passed out, sinking forward and appreciating the dulling of her pain.

An x-ray led to a minor operation to repair a tear in her right lung. The tear caused blood to pool and contributed to Lara’s considerable pain.

“Just a tiny tear and a minor operation,” the registrar informed her with a smile. “Happens all the time with broken ribs, especially there.”

Kerry responded to the doctor’s white coat with wide eyed awe. Young, blond, and muscular, he ticked all her boxes. Lara tried not to smirk as she postured and flirted with him. The confines of the tiny, curtained cubicle did little to spoil her game, but he proved far too young for her. He brushed off Kerry’s efforts without faltering. “The bruising masked the bleeding at first, but we picked up this tear on the CT scan. Sometimes they heal without intervention but it’s not worth the risk. A big cough can cause it to burst apart.”

Remembering his bedside manner and putting aside his enclosed-space-flirt-a-thon with Kerry, he paused. Lara covered her eyes with her hand. “Can you stop now?” she begged. “It’s best I don’t know all the details.”

"How does it feel now?" he asked her. He frowned as Kerry sauntered next to him. She bumped a trolley with her hip and it rolled into the next cubicle, taking the curtain with it.

"Like somebody danced the Hallelujah Chorus on my ribcage," Lara replied with a groan.

"That's good," the doctor replied, distracted by the sight of Kerry chasing the trolley. "But you've done your dash with the morphine now, so it's good old codeine and paracetamol for you."

"Fantastic," Lara replied under her breath, grateful for whatever the nurse just stuck into the cannula. If it proved her last drug hit, she'd enjoy the ride.

The doctor shimmied away, looking over his shoulder at Kerry until he walked into a medicine trolley. He straightened it as his cheeks pinked and he scurried away with haste. But the nice nurse with the awesome chemicals returned and Lara smiled with hope in her eyes.

Unfortunately, she brought Arama in tow. "Lara what happened?" He plonked his tall frame on the bed, only just avoiding the cannula lead. The nurse looked nervous. Arama's distinctive looks jarred with his unpredictable behaviour. His elegant head whipped round, and he jabbed a long finger in Kerry's seated direction. "You should have told me! Catharine asked *me* to look after her."

Kerry shook her head. "No! Catharine asked *me* to look after her!"

"Actually," the nurse interjected with an authoritative tone, "neither of you are looking after her very well at the moment." She turned back to Lara asking her, "Is there anything I can get you?"

Lara's eyes seemed to lose their focus and her vision blurred. As the medication took hold, she watched the room spin. Her words slurred. "I think I'd like a different selection of visitors," she managed as faces bloomed and disappeared.

The nurse smiled and Arama and Kerry looked hurt. Lara didn't see any of it as she attempted to drag one of her reluctant eyes away from perusing the ceiling. As her friends picked up their bickering once again, Lara had the overwhelming desire to beg Kerry not to mention her Māori heritage to Arama, but what emerged from her mouth was something different. A bizarre thought took root within her drugged brain and it seemed to present an answer for her friends' dislike of one another. It was ludicrous, but Lara voiced it anyway. Waving her incompetent arm in the general direction of Arama's deep, melodious voice, Lara pointed and shouted, "You're Father Christmas!"

Chapter Eight

"It's ok, she's joking. I'm not. I'm really not," Arama pleaded for the hundredth time to the gaggle of visiting children who collected at the end of the bed. "He's small and fat and I'm too tall." Arama patted his trim stomach, while Kerry tried not to wet herself in the visitor's chair wedged between the curtain and the night stand. The children eyed one another, unconvinced. So Arama played his trump card. "I'm brown. Father Christmas is white. I don't look good in red."

He realised his terrible mistake as a little African boy wearing a red tee shirt suffered every eye of the gathering crowd turning in his direction. Then he ran off back to his family in a hail of tears. Kerry sounded like she was in pain, twisting up in the chair as though being wrung out. "You're such a moron," she spluttered.

"At least I'm not your ex-husband," Arama hissed, touching Lara's delicate fingers with his own. "Why would she think that?"

"No idea," Kerry guffawed, trying to get herself together. "But visiting time is now over, you're about to get lynched by that family for destroying their child's life and I need a ride home."

"Good luck with that!" Arama spat.

The nurse returned to eject the troublemakers. Arama rose in obedience, cringing beneath the nurse's curious stare. His brow furrowed as he stroked the comatose Lara's hand one last time and stood up straight, his white shirt rumpled.

"Oh!" Realisation dawned on the nurse's face and she bit her lip. "I saw you on TV the other night. You invented that piece of software which can..."

"You were on TV?" Kerry's head whipped round so fast she almost gave herself whiplash. "Why? Did you murder someone?"

"No!" The nurse's eyes glittered with excitement. "He invented this piece of software which..."

Kerry finished her sentence. "I bet he murdered someone in America. That's why he came back." She jabbed a finger at him. "Just when I hoped you'd gone for good with your perfectly aligned wheely bins and your perfect blinds and your perfect everything." Kerry's rant halted at the appearance of the distraught child's sister. She approached the dangerous knot of visitors hoping to clarify something important. She jerked her head at Arama but spoke to Kerry.

"So, is he not Father Christmas then?"

Kerry shook her head with exaggerated sadness, while the whole bay full of patients and retreating visitors watched and listened through a gap in the curtains. "No," she said with an enormous sigh. "He killed him."

The child ran away emitting a high-pitched wail. The nursing manager ejected the sleeping Lara's visitors. A bitter wind whipped up floating snowflakes in the car park and Kerry faced the prospect of calling a taxi. Upsetting Arama removed her last hope of a free lift. She wandered over to the bus shelter and looked at the timetable. At least she had her purse with her.

The sound of a vehicle pulling up alongside her grabbed her attention and Arama's dark, brooding face peered out from his shiny black Audi. "Just get in!" he snapped.

Kerry thought about it for a moment, but a gentle flurry of snow drifted over her like a haze and the timetable declared the next bus wouldn't be for another half an hour. She pulled the door open with laboured movements and sat in the plush upholstery, feeling wrong-footed.

"You should have told me. I caused it," Arama griped, having said nothing until they reached the pretty village of Rothwell. He seethed behind brooding, dark eyes.

"She didn't want me to tell you anything," Kerry retorted, sounding tired. She rubbed at her eyes with a slender hand, noticing mascara residue on her fingers when she finished.

"Why?" Arama demanded.

Kerry's tiredness caught up with her and stopped her brain engaging with her mouth. "She didn't want you to know anything about her. Not at all. I don't understand why, but she was adamant I didn't tell you she was M..." *Shut up Kerry, shut up Kerry, shut up stupid woman.* The dull mantra forced her lips closed. Arama looked across at her in horror, fumbling his turn off the roundabout and almost running into a slowing lorry.

"She's married?" His face darkened and something clicked in Kerry's tired brain. She saw a chance to hurt the rude, arrogant male but for once, didn't take it. In her best teacher's voice, she tried to make things less fraught.

"It's none of your business. Or mine. I won't discuss this with you anymore. If you let me out here, I'm sure I can get a bus."

Arama blasted through Rothwell as though it was a racetrack. People scattered left and right and Kerry marvelled he didn't get pulled over by a cop. The car blew straight past the bus stop and she suppressed her relief. Despite not enjoying the journey, she didn't want to wait for the bus much either.

"What else begins with, 'm' if it's not 'married'?" she heard Arama mutter under his breath.

Chapter Nine

The nursing staff wouldn't let Lara walk to the bus stop. In fact, the doctor refused to discharge her into the care of the transport service at all, despite her protestations she had cash and would be fine. Lara thought about the little Fiesta in the garage at home. She hadn't run it as often as Catherine asked, because everything she needed lay within walking distance. "This is your punishment," she grumbled.

In the end, it was Arama who turned up to fetch her after a row with Kerry the previous night. It resembled a childish spat over a glass of wine. "I'll get Lara."

"No, I'll get her."

"You can't just walk out of class; I'll get her."

And so it went. After the dreadful hospital visit and the fraught ride home, Arama parked in the garage behind his house. Not wanting to negotiate the ridiculous five-minute walk round to the front of her own house, Kerry walked through his, stopping on the way for a glass of merlot and an argument. "Is it because I made a pass at you at Catharine's New Year's party that time?" Kerry demanded. "I was quite drunk if you remember. Is that why you don't like me?"

"No!" Arama bit back. "That's nothing to do with it. I get women throwing themselves at me all the time. I'm used to it!"

Kerry was furious with his arrogance. 2012 was a dreadful year. Mr Christmas had been - and still was - a headteacher at another local primary school. He became rather too fond of his bursar and ditched Kerry, confessing everything at her thirty-fifth birthday party. The divorce came through just before Christmas, and the settlement. She kept the house and the mortgage. He got the mutton dressed as lamb and the sympathy of their joint friends. "Fine!" Kerry muttered, swigging the last of her wine and feeling smug about the flakes of mud she clumped through from the garage and sprinkled along Arama's laminate flooring. And then they got into a row about who would fetch Lara, ending with Kerry retorting, "I have no idea how Catharine copes with having to work with you. I find it hard to believe you're successful in business. She must have to keep you on a leash to stop you chewing up her customers."

"They're not her customers; they're *our* customers. It's a joint company and yes, thank you, offices all over the world are proof of outstanding success. *I'll* fetch Lara."

It was too late. Kerry was already out on the doorstep as Arama slammed the painted navy front door in her face. The brass knocker with the majestic lion's head wobbled on its hinge. Kerry did an ungracious 'v' sign at the closed door and then turned it into a nose-scratch, in case any of the street's school children looked through their front windows. News of something like that would rip through the community quicker than her husband's affair.

The nursing staff eyed Arama with suspicion the next day. Tall, smart and imposing, he masked his good looks with a brusque and officious manner. They'd fielded complaints from the day before after his unfortunate statements about 'Santa.' But Lara already waited in the day room with a single carrier bag at her feet. It limited the damage he could do.

"Oh, hi," Lara said, rising from the high-backed chair with difficulty. "Did they call you? They wouldn't let me catch the bus."

Arama shook his head and gave an impatient flap of his hand. Lara imagined it was a dreadful inconvenience for him to leave the office. She realised she didn't know where he worked and hoped he wouldn't get into trouble for playing hooky on her behalf. He tutted as a nurse called them back to the reception desk so that Lara could collect her previously withheld discharge envelope.

"Are you staying with her?" the nurse asked. "We can't let her go if she's going home alone."

Arama opened his mouth to speak, closing it with a snap as Lara administered a kick to the ankle with her sharp boot. "Yes, he is." She smiled and accepted the envelope.

Arama looked even crosser if that were possible and stumped down the corridor after her.

Sleet crunched underfoot, and the sky held less grey than when Lara entered the hospital. She inhaled a heavy sigh of pleasure at the cold fresh air. A painful bout of coughing ensued, and she clutched her chest and limited her intake. Arama displayed hidden empathy, slipping his hand beneath Lara's elbow and supporting her as she groaned and hacked.

"Steady," he soothed. "Take smaller breaths." He stroked her back with extreme care.

Even after the pain subsided and Lara hauled her sorry backside over to the sleek, black Audi, Arama kept his hand under her arm, his muscles stretching his jacket sleeve taut. Once he had her settled and shut the heavy passenger door, he answered a call on his mobile phone. The air froze on Arama's hair and he offered Lara an apologetic smile. She waved a hand to negate his guilt, and he continued his hurried conversation in stilted answers. His clipped precision made Lara wonder how his co-workers viewed Arama. She realised she didn't even know his second name. Lara watched him sideways from beneath her lashes, embarrassed when he caught her appraising him.

His voice contained an edge of authority. Hone would have called it *mana*, or that elusive spiritual quality Māori sought. It proved powerful and heady in such close proximity. Lara recognised sensations in her chest which needed shutting down in haste. Arama ended the call without even saying goodbye to the female voice on the other end.

He drove the miles to Market Harborough with care, eyeing Lara sideways as he negotiated corners and roundabouts. She forced a smile onto her lips, staring through the window at the blurred green landscape. "It's so different here, isn't it?" she sighed. Arama glanced at her with an unreadable expression on his face. Lara warbled on, growing more uncomfortable by the second at the odd atmosphere that crept into the vehicle. She knew she should shut up, but didn't like being told what to do by that wise, inner voice. "The sky is so huge in New Zealand, but the countryside seems softer and somehow friendlier here. Have you ever been there?"

Lara knew just by the stiffness of Arama's body language she had 'lit the blue touch paper,' 'popped the grenade pin,' call it what you will. She caused something to detonate in the man's psyche. "Of course I've been there! I grew up there until I was ten. It's a God-forsaken place if ever there was one and I hate it!"

The heated air in the vehicle seemed to crowd around Lara's face as she broke out into a sweat. *I'm in the car with a lunatic*; she repeated to herself. She tried not to panic as she caught sight of the little vein that ticked furiously in the side of Arama's neck just above his pristine white shirt collar. The dark bottom of his tie poked out underneath the starched material, taunting his habitual perfectionism as though waving to Lara and making her complicit in his dishevelment. Lara tried to distract herself for the rest of the journey, by working out what the male equivalent of a 'bunny boiler' might be. Everything she thought of seemed to come out macho and so she decided a male weirdo would have to be a 'bunny boiler' as well. She hoped Marble was still intact when she got home, but figured Arama liked Catharine, even if he hated her. Besides which, Marble was a fat and very scratchy cat, not a soft, harmless bunny rabbit and Catharine didn't own a saucepan large enough to fit him in.

Arama parked in his garage and Lara dragged herself out of the car. Coming home from the hospital was exhausting in a not-actually-doing-anything-kind-of-way. The garage door was automatic unlike Catharine's, which demanded Lara dangled from a cord to close it. Shelving racks covered every wall, stocked with tools and gadgets. A small white label stuck to the front of each shelf denoted its contents. His compulsiveness added another quirk to his personality and Lara turned away to smirk.

Arama led her through the back of the house and she found herself in a modern, spotless stainless steel kitchen.

She declined a drink, desperate to get home and lie down on the bed. Missing the social queues, her companion accompanied her out into the street and in through the front door of her home. He moved around Catharine's kitchen with obvious familiarity, making her a cup of tea that she wanted, but wouldn't have made for herself.

Upstairs in the bedroom, Lara's pale and haggard appearance shocked her in the ensuite mirror. After taking a warm shower, she dressed in her comfiest pyjamas. She appeared from the bathroom looking peachy pink, her hair tangled and fluffy on her head. It hung down her back like curly black silk. She got the gauze dressing on her chest damp. It itched beneath her pyjama top, but she yawned with exhaustion and decided not to care.

"Oh." She jumped with shock to find Arama standing in front of her bedroom window. With his hands deep in his pockets, he stared through the glass without seeing. Lara cleared her throat and her gaze edged towards her bed. She craved sleep more than anything else.

Arama turned to greet her. For a moment the dark shadow left his face as he smiled. Lara's heart lurched in her chest like a boulder flung into the depths of a lake.

"I hung around to check you were ok. There's a pot of tea in case you want a drink. I'll go home soon." He looked around the room as though searching for something and Lara waited for his cool assurance to return. It didn't.

"Please can you pour me a drink?" she asked, wincing at the feebleness of her voice. Arama nodded and walked towards the tray he'd laid on the dressing table. He flicked the switch on the wall television and tossed the remote control onto the bed.

"I'm not sure if you like daytime TV," he said, his tone serious. The comforting music of a soap opera drifted into the room. He shot a glance over his shoulder and Lara recalled their first meeting and his disgust at her jetlag as she sat in front of the television.

She settled onto the bed and pulled a fluffy blanket over herself. The comfy mattress enfolded her, giving her permission to spend time in bed during the day. "Don't you want a cup?" she asked, noticing only one mug on the tray. He hesitated and then nodded. Lara heard him walk downstairs, open a cupboard in the kitchen and then return at a faster pace.

Lara woke two hours later. She snuffed around, struggling to rouse herself in the warmth of the blanket. The gentle stroke of fingers ran through her hair, reaching the end of a curl and starting over again. Shrouded in safety, she dozed for a while longer. When she woke again, her tongue stuck to the roof of her mouth. An object dug into her cheek, the sensation causing an ache to blossom outwards and snake around her head. Her breathing hitched and the dull ache awoke in her chest.

Lara forced herself upright, scrabbling at the mattress. Instead, her fingers gripped a shirt and hard muscle. "Steady," Arama said. His light tone confused her, and she groaned.

"Why are you here?" she demanded, her voice overloud. She stuck out her tongue and screwed up her face.

"You fell asleep and didn't swallow your antibiotic." Arama used both hands to slide himself up the mattress until his head leaned against the pillows. "I bet your mouth feels gross."

Lara rubbed her eyes. "It does. Did you fall asleep?" She peeked from beneath her lashes.

"No." Arama yawned. "You laid on my stomach and I couldn't relax."

Lara tutted and considered offering an apology. Her shoulders stiffened, and she turned away to screw up her face again at the plastic taste on her tongue.

Arama's presence heightened her sense of vulnerability. His hand rested against her spine as she knelt up to study him. An expression of peace and contentment shuttered in less than a second, hidden from her view.

A soccer game played out on the television and Lara turned her attention to the green and red players while she worked out a coherent sentence. Arama sat up in a fluid movement, using his stomach muscles. He ran his index finger over her cheek, his touch gentle. "Sorry," he whispered. "My belt buckle dug into your face."

"It's fine." Unable to cope with her confusion, Lara pushed herself off the bed and went into the bathroom. She closed the door and leaned against it. Footsteps crossed her bedroom twice, and she held her breath, waiting for Arama to leave.

Her bathroom door opened with a creak and her fingers trembled. She entered her empty bedroom with a sigh of feigned relief. Downstairs, Arama replaced the tea tray, opening and closing the dishwasher once. Lara tapped her fingers against her thigh but chose not to prolong the awkwardness. She walked down the stairs and prepared to thank him for his neighbourly help.

"Don't you need to get back to work?" she asked him, resting against the kitchen door frame. "Thanks for your help."

"Would you like me to go?" Arama stopped to study her, and Lara struggled.

"No. Yes. No. I don't know."

He laughed and her insides did an unhelpful flip which proved painful. He shrugged. "I'll wait while you decide. He reached for the teapot and emptied out the dregs. As the kettle boiled, he added more teabags and retrieved two clean mugs.

"Do you feel better?" he enquired, placing the teapot on the table. "You slept for a couple of hours."

Lara sighed and settled into a chair. "I need to go to work on Wednesday."

Arama frowned. "They can't expect you back so soon," he interjected.

She shook her head. "I hope they don't find out about this. They're employing me for a specific role on a limited budget. I can't afford to miss days and waste time."

"I wish some of my staff showed that much dedication." Arama raised an eyebrow and Lara's cheeks reddened. "What's your role at the museum," he asked.

Lara's lips parted in an instant apology. Angela trusted her to keep the discovery secret. She searched for a polite answer that wouldn't sound evasive. "I make sure historical items last long enough to give clarity to future generations. Every artifact has a story to tell. They can't do that if they're lost, damaged or worse. I digitise them, catalogue them and give them a place in history."

Arama snorted, his brown eyes flashing in his face with a curious pain. "What could be worse than being lost or damaged?"

"Obscurity," Lara answered with confidence. "A once precious item without its provenance or history just becomes another historical bauble with no place. It's not just about monetary value, but about what the object tells us about our ancestors. Take paintings for example. When I worked at the Tate, I witnessed incredible works by painters and sculptors who could create something alive with their talent. I saw cornfields I wanted to run through and horses I could reach out and stroke. But the most important feature wasn't the work itself, but the artist's biography. It's this curious circular existence. The more intriguing or colourful an artist is, the more desperate people become for their work. Have you never noticed that?"

Arama gave a slow, calculated nod. Passion for her craft poured from Lara's eyes and her skin glowed as though back lit by an ethereal flame. Arama froze in the cross hairs of her fire, paralysed and in awe. Until her excitement made her careless. "My last job involved a family history. There were trinkets and photos and a diary."

Grief and loss washed over Lara as the words left her lips. They flayed the open wound of her heart. She silenced and Arama watched her through narrowed eyes. "Thanks for the tea," he said, as though forgetting he'd made it. He rose to leave and Lara followed him along the hallway to the front door. Hone's possessions screamed at her from the secret safe under the bottom step and she deafened herself to its cry.

Arama pushed his feet into his shoes and squatted down to lace them. He looked at her with his unreadable dark expression on his face. As Lara prepared to thank him again for his help, he delivered a painful volley. "Has it ever occurred to you, Lara, that what you do for a living isn't always best for everyone concerned? You think the past should have a voice and display its wares for all to see. But some of us would rather keep our history hidden. We like it that way."

He turned to leave, his muscles bulging through his shirt sleeves. The prong of his belt buckle remained sticking up, reminding Lara of the ache on her cheek. Arama snatched his jacket off the peg behind the door and hesitated. They both reached for the door handle at the same moment, Arama keen to leave and Lara desperate to get rid of him.

A strange electrical chemistry passed between them as their fingers collided, confirming what they each already knew. A latent passion lurked just beneath the surface, surging with every passing encounter.

"Lara," Arama whispered, as though tasting her name. He reached for her cheek, running his thumb over the reddened mark left by his belt buckle. Danger surged like a tidal wave, robbing Lara of speech or movement.

Arama's fingers strayed along her jawline and into her hair, creating a rush of warmth. Her stomach tingled as his lips pressed against the red groove in her cheek. "I'm sorry," he whispered, part apology and part confusion.

Lara tasted the heady scent of expensive aftershave as his lips moved across hers. He intoxicated her, filling her nose and the back of her throat with his potent maleness. Rough bristles rasped against her cheek and scratched her chin. Arama edged her back against the wall, dropping his jacket to the floor as his arms encircled her waist.

Lara splayed her hands against the wall behind her, the textured wallpaper alive beneath her palms. As his mouth moved against hers, she parted her lips and heard him sigh.

But he hadn't earned her trust. As he clasped her closer and his kiss deepened, Lara held her breath. She waited for the dark presence in him to rise again, tossing its head like a stallion freed from a coral. His lips moved to her cheek and then her neck, delicate kisses increasing in pressure. Lara's stomach clenched as though she'd swung too high. She bit her lip to stop the gasp from escaping.

"Sorry, sorry." Arama took a step back and dropped his hands. "I shouldn't have done that." He cleared his throat and bent to snatch up his jacket. He said the words but didn't seem sorry enough, kissing her again before wrenching open the front door with a curse.

Then he left, taking the front steps two at a time and swinging out of the gate. Lara pushed the door closed behind him and leaned against the wall, more confused than she'd ever felt.

Chapter Ten

"Sorry Love, but this parcel won't go through the letterbox next door. It's too wide, and it says, '*Please don't bend.*' It's made it this far, so it seems a shame to just shove it through the gap. Looks like the poor thing's been halfway round the world."

Lara looked at the wide, brown envelope in the postman's hands as though it had the power to destroy her world.

Because it did.

It already had.

She reached out to take it from him and then dropped her hands. "Why is it here?" she demanded. "This isn't where it should have gone."

"Dunno love." The postman shrugged. An Artic blast created a growing drip on the end of his frozen nose. "Can you take it?" he asked, cocking his head.

Lara stared at the brown envelope. Her heart hammered the blood through her eardrums like a jazz beat. She shook her head. "This isn't where it's meant to be," she whispered. She took a step backwards, and the postman shoved it into her arms.

"There's extra to pay," he said, eyeing her with caution. "Not enough stamps."

Lara's eyes widened. "That's because it's come to the wrong place!" She raised her voice, and the parcel tipped, slipping from the ledge of her folded arms. She caught it one handed, and the postman smiled with satisfaction. "That's another four pounds and fifty pence," he said with a flapping hand. "They put the new address on the label, but didn't say why. For future reference, there's no charge if they write 'no longer at this address' or something of that ilk." He jerked his head at the parcel. "But they didn't."

Lara stared down at the brown wrapper, small tears and greasy patches marking its journey. The postman looked back towards the gate and then at her again. He repeated his question. "Can you settle up? I can take cash." He winced. "Or I can take it back to the depot. They'll destroy it."

Lara yelped and clutched the parcel to her breast. "No! I'll just get my purse." She set it on the hall cupboard and retrieved her handbag from the bottom step. "Her fingers fumbled out a five-pound note, and she thrust it into his outstretched hand and slammed the door.

"What about your change?" He flipped open the letterbox and his eyes stared at her through the gap. "I owe you fifty pence."

"Keep it!" Lara shouted. She snatched up the parcel and took it into the lounge, closing the door behind her. Moments later, the gate clicked as the postman proceeded on his way.

Relief sent the adrenaline roaming free through her bloodstream and Lara gasped. She sank down against the lounge door until her bottom touched the floor. The sobs came thick and fast, as desolation, grief and frustration mingled in her chest. Her tears ran over the battered address label, causing her handwriting to become illegible as the black ink absorbed the salt water. The dark line scribed through Lara's neat label had redirected the envelope from Mr A Livingstone in a New York office to the house next door.

To Arama.

Lara sat on the floor until her leg muscles trembled with cold and inactivity. Her arms ached from holding the stiff brown envelope too hard and she'd bent it despite the printed instruction. She didn't open the envelope, already intimately familiar with its well-travelled contents. She'd placed every one of them there, sealed against harm and sent with best wishes from a whole other life.

The house shook with the vibration of a door slamming. Lara started and the painful hitch in her chest released as a hiccup. Grief turned to rage in less than a second and she hauled herself up from the ground like an elderly woman. Wrenching the front door open and leaving it gaping wide, she ran through her front gate and barged Arama's open with force. She hammered on his door with the heel of her hand, sending darts of pain shooting through her wrist. After a lifetime of waiting and more hammering, the door disappeared from in front of her. She'd put so much anger into her knocking, she fell forwards into the entrance, the parcel still clutched between her forearm and chest. Bare chested and wearing only a pair of shorts, he dangled a tee shirt from his left hand.

"Whoa!" Arama caught her as she tipped. His arm against her ribs caused a gasp of pain to echo off the brickwork.

"Get off me!" she yelled at him, slapping his hands until she'd righted herself. The tee shirt fluttered onto the carpet. “Leave me alone!”

Arama tilted his head and squinted at her. His lips slid open into a line of sarcasm. “You knocked on my door.” He peered around her and snorted. “And you bust the hinge on my gate.”

“You!” She raised her index finger and jabbed it against his muscular chest. “You!”

“Okay.” Arama nodded to a woman pushing a pram along the street. He seized Lara’s wrist and dragged her into the house before slamming the door behind him. “What is wrong with you?” he demanded.

Lara slammed the parcel against his bare chest. Another crease appeared across the centre, enraging her even more.

A gentle dusting of hair covered his pectorals, snaking in a line over his stomach and into his shorts. Lara struggled for control, shoving at the parcel to force Arama to take its weight. “I’ve bent it now!” she yelled into his face, aware she’d pulverised it on the shortest leg of its journey. She’d been the first and last person to handle it, the irony painful. “Take it!” she hissed at him through gritted teeth.

Arama looked down at the address label and frowned. He noticed the Royal Mail sticker and the additional cost. He shrugged. “I’ll pay you back,” he said, his lips turning upwards in confusion. “No need to rip your nightie over four quid.” He raised a speculative eyebrow. “But that’s not the problem between us, is it?”

Lara groaned. “It was you!” she hissed. “You’re Arie Hohaia. You’re Hone’s grandson.” Tears coursed unchecked down her blotchy face as she failed to regain command of herself. Her self-control had sneaked back through the broken gate and she should have followed it. “He loved you!” she screamed. “He did it all for you. Two years of cataloguing and photographing, labelling and writing your family history. For an ungrateful, self-centred man who didn't deserve any of it. Your rejection killed him! He dreamed of meeting you, his lost grandson. He talked about you every day for two years and this is who you are? I'm so glad that noble old man never had the misfortune to meet you. It would have broken his heart like it's broken mine."

Lara turned to leave, taking one last look at the chunky brown envelope. She'd filled it with Hone, such hope and excitement involved in its compilation. "I hope the contents of that envelope break you into a million pieces, because it's what you deserve," she snarled. "Stay away from me. Don't talk to me and don't come near me. I never want to see your miserable face again as long as I live!"

Then she left, slamming both his front door and her own.

Arama stood in his hallway still clutching the envelope to his chest, his fingers trembling. He He heard Lara's muffled sobs drift through the thin wall from next door but couldn't move. The thing in his hands filled him with terror. And regret.

Kerry attendance at a parents' evening meant she wouldn't call around for a chat. It also meant she didn't witness Lara's destruction. Grief rode her like a rodeo champion, digging its cruel spurs into her damaged heart and not releasing her until she'd collapsed. By the time she sank into a tortured fitful sleep, she knew she'd never find happiness again. *Of course, he was Hone's grandson,* she chided herself. *That was the attraction.*

Though he hadn't known it, Arama carried the old man's genetics. He lacked the ready smile and the wicked chuckle, though she'd sensed they existed beneath his gruff, humourless exterior. Lara felt Hone's loss again as though it had emerged from the freezer like frozen peas, as fresh as the day of packaging.

Her empty bedroom in all its opulence offered no answers. No sound came through the wall from next door and Lara conjured up mental images of Arama's evening. Had he opened the parcel, or cast it onto the sofa or into the dustbin?

"Hone's grandson," she whispered into the darkness. "You broke that old man's heart and he relinquished his grasp on life as if you'd pushed him off a cliff. I hate you." Lara sniffed against her pillow. "I hate you."

But that was the problem. She didn't.

Chapter Eleven

Lara arrived at work early the next morning. Her eyes resembled something a bullfrog might be proud of, but she sat in her darkened room and dusted, wrapped and catalogued until her brain hurt. Somehow, reading the notes made by a man in hiding whose words betrayed a naked fear for his life, consoled and reminded her of her mission. *This* was her calling, to document the truth about history. It wasn't her problem what the council decided to do with the knowledge after she'd finished.

Angela visited Lara with enquiries about her progress. She didn't understand the processes required to heal such precious things and frowned as she concentrated.

"Look," Lara said, handling the oldest diary with gentle, gloved fingers. "I've got rid of the dust. Can you see the detail in the pages better now?"

"Yes." Angela pursed her lips and exhaled. "What's next?"

"I've documented each of them, dating them by the events they describe. There's a company in London which specialises in scanning artifacts. They have a special cradle which hangs beneath the copier, so they don't need to crack the delicate spines. I thought I'd take them there."

Angela's eyes bugged. "Heck, yes. You'll need to take them personally. We can't risk sending them with a courier." She flicked a red nailed finger towards the flaking leather on one manuscript. "Can they fix that?"

Lara winced. "We don't fix things because it destroys their provenance. The rule is to do no harm. That's what I'm working towards; cleaning them enough to make them readable, but not damaging them more than the rain already did. This one isn't as bad as the one we found on top. It protected all the ones beneath it, but took the brunt of the damp through the sack cloth."

"How expensive is this London company?" Angela winced. "The councillors gave me a secret budget, but it's limited. They're hoping to recoup any investment through publicity and exhibitions."

Lara cocked her head. "I should advise you again to contact the National Archives. These manuscripts are a treasure for the whole country. We may have already contravened the legislation relating to the Queen's Treasure Trove." She bit her lip, knowing her advice fell on deaf ears.

Angela dismissed it with a predictable wave of her hand. "We will," she promised. "But not yet. Get me a quote from the company and I'll allocate a purchase order." She lifted a finger to her lips to assert her request for confidentiality. "You're sure this company can keep a secret?"

Lara nodded. "I can vouch for them. We used them all the time at the Tate."

"What will you do with that one?" Angela pointed to the sorriest exhibit.

Lara's eyes widened. "I can't do anything with it. I'm an archivist, not a restorer. When I take the others to

London, I'll drop into the Tate and see if my old colleagues have any suggestions. It's just an extra stop on the Underground."

The fragility of the manuscript deterred Lara even from parting the binding to peek inside it. She suspected it continued the story which began in the first journal and forced herself to curb her curiosity. The priests' tale would keep for another time when she could savour it without damaging the relic.

Working on the manuscripts satiated her dreadful ache for emotional closure, helping her to push her own private agonies to the back of her mind. Lara expended all her energy on their care, leaving herself with nothing available for despair at the end of each day. As Christmas marched nearer, Kerry involved herself in the annual nativity play and relieved Lara of the torturous Monday art class. Her evenings involved entertaining a new male colleague who seemed enamoured with her. Lara caught sight of him once from the bedroom window and spied the wine bottles in Kerry's recycling bin on rubbish day.

Lara may have experienced a sense of abandonment, had numbness not occupied her soul. She walked from work to home, wasted the time in between, and then returned to work again. When Kerry cancelled their Monday art class, she worked for free on the manuscripts instead.

Arama left two weeks earlier and didn't make contact. Lara watched him leave the house the day after her screaming fit. He used the back entrance from Nithsdale Avenue, crossing the car park towards Welland Park. She hadn't seen him since. She wondered if he'd returned to New York and intended to stay away until after she'd left the town. Part of her hoped so, while the other part grieved.

The slam of Arama's front door one Saturday morning sent her shooting from her armchair. A man and woman left through his front gate after glancing up at the windows. Concerned, she phoned Kerry.

"Hey." Kerry yawned and Lara heard her shuffling around as though still bed. A male voice rumbled in the background and she cringed.

"Sorry. Didn't mean to wake you. It doesn't matter." Lara prepared to end the call.

"Don't be daft." Kerry yawned again. "We had a late night making scenery. I should have asked for your help. My donkey looks like a mutant. What's wrong?"

Lara exhaled. "I just saw a couple leaving Arama's house. Both in their early sixties, maybe. The woman wore a long coat and her white hair in a bun. They must have had a key. I didn't know whether or not to call the police." Another thought occurred to her, and she groaned. "Oh, don't worry. I just realised he might have put the house up for sale. Maybe they're prospective buyers."

Kerry tutted. "No, don't worry. It sounds like his parents. I've met them. They're far too nice to have produced someone as horrid as him. I think they picked up the wrong baby at the hospital."

"But they're white," Lara said. She winced and added, "Not that their skin colour matters."

Kerry snorted. "Like I said, they must have grabbed the wrong baby. Somebody else has their nice, respectable son with the good manners and generous spirit. Arama would behave like an idiot regardless of his skin colour."

"Ok, thanks. Enjoy your Saturday." Lara ended the call and went back to her novel. The door slammed again later, and she ignored the sound of occupancy next door.

Aunt Catharine expected to arrive home in early April. Lara's temporary contract at the museum ended just after Christmas, but the speed at which she worked predicted she'd finish much sooner. "I can't keep living from week to week," she told Marble as he jumped into her lap with a mewl. "It might be time to move on. Maybe Kerry will take responsibility for you if I secure a job before Aunt Catherine gets home."

Lara planned her business trip to London for the second week in December. It seemed a foolish time to immerse herself in the capital's Christmas frenzy, but she took advantage of her friend's downturn in workload to trust her with the digitisation of the manuscripts. Lara looked forward to seeing the Christmas lights, but with nobody to buy presents for she planned to avoid the busy commercial parts of the city.

"You're only going for one night?" Kerry frowned as she accepted the spare door key and instructions for feeding Marble. "It hardly seems worth it. Why don't you visit Harrods and some of the boutique stores." She closed her eyes and leaned her head back on her shoulders. "I just love London at Christmas. My favourite are the lights on Oxford Street."

Lara smiled and gave her a wave. Her tiny suitcase skittered behind her on the pavement, containing the manuscripts and her overnight clothes.

It took fifty minutes for the fast train to travel from the station at Market Harborough to London, St. Pancreas. But Lara experienced a culture shock as she fought her way through dense foot traffic to the to the Underground line she needed. Jaunty Christmas music blared from every speaker and London heaved with milling bodies. A burly man tripped over Lara's case and swore at her as he tried to overtake her in a queue. She maintained her grip on the heavy bag, hoping he hadn't damaged the artifacts.

She arrived at the Tate Gallery moments before the agreed time. The huge stone steps up to the entrance filled her with mixed emotions. She paused to run her fingers down one of the wide bricks next to the front doors. Memories of her father rose in her inner vision, bringing with them pain and overwhelming loss. She'd run to New Zealand and back again, but the image had remained on the steps waiting for her.

During his cancer treatment, her father often caught the Tube to meet her for lunch. He'd bought a variety of sandwiches from different cafes on his way back from chemo, enjoying the food by proxy once his appetite abandoned him. Lara had eaten and chatted, believing he'd recover long past the point where the evidence foretold a different outcome.

She missed him with a heartrending ache and pressed her fingers to her lips to contain the wail of misery. She beat it back, the buried emotion and sense of loss retreating for now. Then she walked up the wide, familiar steps and into the gallery, bumping her suitcase behind her.

The fading spectre of her father turned to watch, his eyes sad and his olive skin pale.

Once inside the gallery, Lara breathed out a sigh of relief. As familiar to her as Aunt Catherine's lounge, it felt like coming home. For the first time in a long while, Lara smiled.

A new member of staff worked the ticketing desk and greeted her with a smile. "Are you here for the Matisse exhibition?" she asked.

Lara shook her head. She swallowed and forced a brusqueness into her tone. "I'm here to see the curator," she said. "Please can you let him know Lara is here?"

Paul Rochelle appeared at speed, his impeccable black suit rustling as he made his way down two levels to greet her. "Lara," he cooed, embracing her. He kissed both of her cheeks and held her at arm's length so he could appraise her. "Beautiful and talented as ever," he said, his voice breathy.

The youngest curator the City of London had ever appointed, Paul Rochelle was a decade shy of his equals. He arrived at the gallery with impressive credentials after a career in France. He kept a possessive arm around Lara's shoulders as he led her towards the lift. "Oh, let me take that," he offered, clasping the suitcase handle in manicured fingers. He towed it along behind him as Lara's high heels clicked along the corridor. "Did that woman from the back blocks pass on my message?" he demanded, eyeing her sideways. They paused at the end and he punched a button on the wall. A muffled whirring began as the lift responded to the summons.

"Back blocks?" Lara frowned.

Paul waved his hand, long fingers cutting through the air. "Somewhere in the north of the country. I can't remember the place. Did she tell you what I said?"

Lara blinked and faltered. She remembered Angela mentioning her references but not her exact words. "I can't recall," she said, her words spilling out too fast.

Paul tutted. "I said I wanted you back here!" His protest held an element of pique. "I asked you to get in touch as soon as possible." The lift doors opened, and he waited for another staff member to move out of the way. "Why would you want to work for a council library doing some menial archiving job when you can work here?" His nose wrinkled with disdain as he dismissed Market Harborough without thought.

Lara's look of instant confusion satisfied him. His arm slipped back around her shoulders. His familiar aftershave enveloped her head, safe, exotic, and demanding. Lara's mind whirled as he contemplated her near miss. Angela hadn't mentioned her New Zealand referee, or her inability to find the executors of Hone's estate. Lara crossed her fingers behind her back and thanked fate for her lucky escape. It seemed Paul's desire to reemploy her had been enough to satisfy Angela of Lara's pedigree.

"It's in Leicestershire," Lara offered. "It's in the, not the north."

"Ah, but is it north of the Watford Gap?" Paul grimaced when Lara nodded. He gave a dramatic shiver. "It's still off the social grid. I went north once." His tone inferred an expedition through a desert tundra. "I couldn't understand a word anyone said."

"Where did you go?" Lara followed him out of the lift and followed him past the first of many exhibitions. She already knew the answer, but Paul loved the telling of his tale. She nodded in all the right places as Paul recounted a dreadful weekend in Northampton. A thirty-minute train ride from London, he told it like he'd crawled on his hands and knees from the borders of Scotland.

Lara struggled with her heavy bag, banging it against her calves and making her tired.

Paul trailed the suitcase, bumping it against his heels as he stopped in front of a Turner. "What have you got in here? Geological rocks from the far north?"

Lara laughed, unable to reply as he gasped with enthusiasm at the next archway. "Oh, my goodness! You must see this. We acquired it as a throwaway. Builders found it in an attic in Soho." He whirled her towards an oil canvas depicting the Madonna and child. The length of his forearm and surrounded by a gilt frame, it had the detail of a Da Vinci. "Took a bloody age to clean. The National Gallery is purple with rage they didn't accept it now. It's worth an absolute mint."

Lara smiled. "Same old Paul. So, the rivalry isn't dead yet then?" She linked her arm through his elbow and matched her step to his as they made their way through the exhibits.

Upstairs in his office, he poured her coffee from a percolator and then sat on the edge of his desk while she sipped the heady brew. "I've missed you," he admitted. "I hate how we parted."

Lara stiffened and stared down into her cup. No words presented themselves which hadn't been said before she left.

"Have you finished with your running away now?" Paul dipped his body, stroking a length of hair away from her face and placing it across her shoulder.

Lara sighed and shook her head. "I'm returning to New Zealand." The sentence spilled from her lips, born of desperation as an excuse but growing in attraction with every moment it remained in the air.

"When?" he demanded. His shoulders rounded and his lips turned down into a pout. He exhaled, flicking at imaginary specks on his expensive pinstriped trousers. "I'll come with you. There must be something I can do over there. Herd sheep or something."

Lara snorted. "That's hilarious, Paul. You'd hate it. People walk around museums in their bare feet. I can imagine your scandalised expression at all those toes trotting next to the exhibits." She sighed. "You think anything without silver service is primitive. I can't see you lasting five minutes."

"Bare feet?" Paul screwed his features into a grimace. "I'd do it for you, Lara. I'd give up everything and follow you. You only have to ask."

"Thank you," Lara said. Her smile lost its humour and became wistful.

"Aw sweetheart," he breathed. His arms encircled her and he wrapped her in his exquisite haze. The suit jacket disguised muscles hewn at the gym and Lara allowed herself for a moment to relax into his embrace. Thoughts of Arama rose unbidden into her mind, filling her with confusion and a spark of anger.

"Is New Zealand in the north?" Paul released her and crow's feet appeared in the corners of his eyes. "I'd hate you to make a liar of me, but I really couldn't go north."

Lara rolled her eyes and sipped her coffee, relieved at having dodged the awkwardness of their reunion. He slapped his thighs and a silver bracelet clanked on his wrist. "Let me take you to dinner tonight. My treat. We can go somewhere plush or somewhere low key. What do you say?"

"Thanks. I'd like that." Lara set her cup on the corner of the desk and leaned forward. "But first, I need some advice about a confidential manuscript."

*****

Lara agreed to meet Paul at a restaurant in China Town later that evening. Armed with a guest pass to the staff areas of the gallery, she trailed her suitcase into the archives. Old colleagues greeted her with enthusiasm and they studied the manuscripts after she swore them to secrecy.

"Have you seen this new chemical?" Lottie asked. She reached across her work bench and retrieved a bottle of mixture which moved like silk when she tipped it. "Why don't you try it on a tiny corner with a bud? It might stop the spread of mildew on the worst of them. You're doing the right thing keeping them at a reduced temperature, but the spores still spread like a wildfire."

Lara hissed through her teeth. "Write down the name for me please. I'll see if the client will source some." Lottie turned the bottle over and jotted down the name of the supplier. Lara caught sight of the price tag and winced. She couldn't imagine Angela sanctioning the exorbitant cost.

"Why doesn't the council pass these onto us?" Lottie asked. She stuffed her pencil into her pocket and handed Lara the note containing the details. "Why employ an archivist and try to keep it in house?" She blinked in horror and winced. "No offence, Lara. You're amazing at what you do. But this job is massive. What do they intend to do with the collection once you've restored it?"

Lara exhaled. "That's above my paygrade," she admitted. "I'm grateful for the work but I'll move on soon." She stroked the uppermost manuscript with her gloved hand. "We all have to let our babies go eventually."

Lottie cocked her head and wrinkled her nose. "Not if you come back here. My babies stay on the walls and come back to Mummy once a year for cleaning."

"Yeah." Lara twisted her lips. "I miss that aspect of it."

Lottie slid her stool from beneath her workbench and slumped onto its worn seat. She picked up a piece of gauze stained with a sepia solution which stank of meths. "Paul would take you back like a shot," she commented as she lost herself in her art again.

At the professional copiers, Lara watched as expert hands lifted the manuscripts one at a time into a suspended cradle. The young man who worked the scanner wore cotton gloves as he worked, parting each page with care. Clear images flew from a printer, packed full of Market Harborough's missing history. "I'll pop copies onto your portable hard drive," he promised.

When he'd completed the task, he helped her to place the manuscripts back into her suitcase.

Lara rode the Underground to the Museum of London at London Wall. She asked for her university friend at the reception desk.

Cilla met her with a delighted smile and led her back into a busy workroom. "I'm so excited to see these manuscripts," she confessed. Red curls swirled around her face and she waggled her eyebrows. "It all sounds a little cloak and dagger though." She watched as Lara lowered her suitcase onto a bench and released the lock holding the zipper closed. "Isn't this something for the Treasure Trove people?"

Lara sighed and pursed her lips. "That's what I keep telling the stakeholder. They don't want to hear it." She lifted the lid of the suitcase to reveal the manuscripts wrapped in their protective cloth. "This is why I need your help." She drew on her gloves and unwrapped the worst of them. "Mildew is affecting the pages. I can't open it any further without causing damage. I've treated the others as best as I could. The Tate staffer suggested a tincture, but it's expensive and I doubt the owner is interested in paying for it. I've reached the end of my limits with how much more I can do for them."

"Are they digitised?" Cilla bent her knees to survey the black spores nestling in the grooves between pages. She didn't reach out to touch the manuscripts.

"Yes," Lara confirmed. "But not this one. I don't want to damage it by hauling it open while it's in this fragile state. I got Hendry's in Fleet Street to scan the others."

"Awesome." Cilla walked three considered paces to the right and then back again. She exhaled and tutted. "I have some ideas, but you'll need to leave it with me."

Lara groaned. "I'll need permission to return without it."

"Give them a call." Cilla jerked her head towards a desk in the corner of the workroom. "A conservative estimate is at least a month to open the pages and treat the mildew. You should tell them the bad news."

Lara nodded. "I suspected as much. She won't be happy." She shrugged. "I guess it's her problem now, anyway. Can I give her your contact details? She'll need to arrange retrieval once you're finished."

Cilla jerked her head back in confusion. "Why? Where are you going?" She brushed loose tendrils of red hair away from her face with her gloved hands and then sighed. Stripping them from long fingers, she dumped them in a box beneath the desk. "Where did you disappear to, anyway? You weren't at the last conference. For what it's worth, I never believed the rumour about the alien kidnapping."

Lara laughed. "Dad spoke with such fondness about New Zealand that after he died, I just wanted to visit. I saw an opportunity and took it. I have a few wrinkles to iron out and then I'm heading back there after Christmas." She swallowed as an image of Hone's possessions called to her from Catherine's safe. Her throwaway comment grew wings, and the idea gained more permanency in her mind.

"Well, good for you!" Cilla squeezed her shoulder and gave her a sad smile. "I wish I had the courage to just get up and go."

Lara grinned. "You should have heard Paul ranting on about the north."

Her friend laughed. "Not the motel story again? Or was it a camping trip? It changes with each retelling, doesn't it?"

She led her back to the entrance, and they hugged before parting. Lara promised she would stay in touch, but they both knew she wouldn't.

London welcomed her with clear skies and Lara drew comfort from the familiarity of the hustle and bustle. But it seemed so impersonal after the closeness of Market Harborough where even the barista in the cafe opposite her office acknowledged her with a smile in the supermarket. The supercity lost its excitement as she battled through crowds, towing the valuable artifacts behind her. As rush hour approached with a vengeance, her suitcase caused multiple pile ups on the Underground. The Harrod's security guard ejected her after demanding to view its contents, behaving as though she'd towed a live bomb into the store.

Lara wished she hadn't opted to stay overnight as the city lost its excited vibe and gave her the cold shoulder. Sadness touched her soul as she fought her way through busy streets and train carriages to her hotel.

After a shower, Lara changed into her evening dress. She secured the manuscripts in the room safe, struggling to fit them all inside the box intended for a laptop and a few personal items.

"We've never lost anything before," the desk clerk assured her. "As long as you set your own code, only our master key can unlock it." She leaned forward and bugged her eyes. "The royal family stay here often."

Lara smiled and turned away to hide her smirk. "Not in the last two centuries," she muttered to herself. She waited with the doorman as her taxi pulled up alongside the front steps and gave the driver the address for her destination in China Town.

Paul had already arrived and clutched a merlot in his manicured fingers. He rose as Lara approached. "I took the liberty of ordering our starter," he said. "I hope you still love fried seaweed." He pressed a kiss to each of her cheeks and waved the server away, holding onto the back of her chair until she'd seated herself. "Haven't you missed this?" he demanded, indicating the restaurant with a wide wave of his arm. Lara smiled without answering.

Outside, China Town bustled as though daylight still commanded the sky. A cosmopolitan version of an Oriental city recreated itself in the sprawling English metropolis. Coloured lights twinkled in the inky darkness and crowds thronged in the street outside the restaurants. Escape called to Lara from another continent, offering her a second chance at healing. But palm leaves and not paper lanterns whispered her name.

She averted her gaze from the windows to find Paul studying her expression. "Stay," he begged, seizing her hand from the tablecloth and stroking her fingers.

Lara pulled her hand from beneath his as the server appeared with their starters. She fought the urge to run screaming from the restaurant and her failed second chance in Harborough, catching the next plane leaving Heathrow.

As Lara savoured an exquisite portion of crispy aromatic duck, her chest prickled with anxiety. Every time she looked up, she found Paul's gaze boring into her face. Their short lived and ill-advised relationship had failed because his affection for himself surpassed anything he'd felt for her. She controlled a sigh of irritation and set her knife and fork together on her plate.

"Aren't you hungry?" His lips turned down into a practiced pout. A strand of blonde hair escaped from his slicked back fringe and he frowned at Lara from beneath it.

"I'll just visit the ladies' room," she said, her heart pounding in her chest. A quick glance around the restaurant revealed satisfied diners tucking into their meals and she rose with a stiff, jerky movement. The server dashed back and hauled away her chair. Lara felt as though everyone turned to observe her. Paul half rose in his seat and gave her a polite bow.

"Shall I order dessert?" he demanded.

Lara floundered. "I'm not sure," she stammered. "Back in a minute."

She steered herself towards the bathroom sign, swerving around tables and avoiding chairs stuck too far into the aisles. Blood pounded in her ears at the realisation if she didn't escape soon, she'd become trapped in a life she no longer wanted. *Coming here was a big mistake,* she chided herself. *There's nothing left for me*. Lara moved across the floor in a lurching motion, halting as a server appeared from the kitchen bearing a platter of steaming rice. She dodged sideways and the tiny hairs rose on the back of her neck, alerting her to an imminent danger. Someone watched her with frightening intensity.

Lara glanced back at Paul as the server passed. Head bent over his plate, he lifted his chopsticks to his lips with expert fingers. He didn't glance in her direction. The other diners had returned their attention to their food, ignoring her as soon as she headed for the bathroom.

"Excuse me, madam." Another server waited behind her, carrying a tray of dirty plates and glasses.

"Sorry," Lara gushed, preparing to move back into the flow of the busy thoroughfare.

Then she glanced up towards the packed mezzanine floor which overlooked the restaurant. Larger tables accommodated the corporate customers and their business parties. A man in a pinstriped suit threw his head back and laughed, a glass of red wine slopping its contents over his fingers.

Lara gasped as the hard, steel rungs of a chair hit the side of her leg with force. Its occupant gaped at her with his mouth open. He'd shot his chair back as he rose to spoon rice from a bowl in the centre of a table. An elderly gentleman leapt from his nearby seat and seized Lara's forearms, apologising on behalf of the embarrassed boy. Seeing the tears begin in the child's eyes, Lara ignored the ache in her thigh and shook her head.

"It's fine, no harm done. Thank you, no, I'm ok," she protested. She wriggled free of his grip and continued her journey towards the bathroom.

She side stepped a raucous group who reached the bottom of the stairs from the mezzanine. They milled around her as loud male voices argued over the bill.

"Lara." She frowned at the sound of the voice and spun, her eyes widening at the sight of Arama waiting on the fringe of the group.

Good sense failed her and she shot him a wide-eyed glance filled with fear, before bolting for the bathroom. Her blood seemed to gutter and choke in her veins, causing light-headedness to wash over her. A heady mix of passion, fury and loss ran through her mind as she burst through the heavy door.

Inside the bathroom, she blew her nose and composed herself. Her fragile equilibrium seemed further away than usual as she considered her reflection in the mirror over the sink. She hardly recognised herself. Flawless makeup masked her pretty features, and she'd lost too much weight in the last year. The emerald evening dress had lost its former snugness, the straps tipping from her slender shoulders like discarded spaghetti. Dark curls tumbled around her face to cascade down her back like a waterfall. *Mum*, her heart cried to her reflection. *When did I become you?*

Forcing the tears back with difficulty, Lara applied lipstick from her tiny clutch bag and pulled her mother's comforting black shawl around her shoulders.

She exited the bathroom, sighing with irritation to find Arama waiting for her. He leaned against the wall as though waiting his turn and blocked Lara's way through the narrow passage. His touch was gentle as he reached for her waist and she registered the faintest tremor in his fingers. "We need to talk," he whispered.

"Leave me alone!" she hissed. She slapped at his forearms and clutched her bag tighter. He dipped his head, and she held her breath, sensing he wished to kiss her. Naked fear flashed in his irises, holding him back from the edge. Lara's heart hammered like a child's toy drum.

Arama's dropped his hands, balling them into fists. He reached for her again and then thought better of it. He performed the same action four times before narrowing his brows into a series of tortured lines. "You don't understand," he began. He took a step backwards and Lara dug her fingers into her ears to block out his words. The simple handbag listed forwards beneath her arm and threatened to fall.

"Please, just listen to me, damn it!" Arama seized her wrists to pull her hands away from her face. "I need to tell you what happened." He ignored Lara's shaking head as he persisted. "I spent the first seven years in foster care, bouncing around the system until my parents adopted me. Why won't you listen to me?" His sentence finished with a plaintive edge.

"Because I don't care!" Lara lied. Her lips parted to spit venom which countered the longing in her heart. But she didn't get to say any of those things.

"What's going on here?" Paul's raised voice echoed along the corridor. He stood behind Arama in his fitted Armani suit, bristling with indignation.

"Who are you?" Arama shot the question in his direction without turning to face him. He dismissed him with consummate ease. "Go away," he bit, not waiting for an answer. "This is a private discussion."

"It looks more of a lecture than a discussion." Paul's hands rested over his hips. It appeared he didn't plan to rescue Lara by traditional means. He frowned and looked back along the corridor as though seeking assistance from someone else. "You need to let her go." He swallowed and took a step closer, calming his expression into one of placation. "She's with me," he said, adding an awkward cackle at the end of the sentence.

Lara seized the opportunity to bat Arama's long fingers aside. She shoved her way between the two men. "I'm leaving," she hissed. "Neither of you should follow me." The clutch bag fell to the tiled floor, and she sighed and retrieved it.

Arama turned his body to face Paul, fury setting his hazel irises on fire. "What are you to Lara?" he demanded.

Paul shrugged and spread his arms. "Well, nothing now, thanks to you." He slapped his thighs in an expression of irritation. "I guess you're the reason she's no longer interested in me. Thanks for driving her back to New Zealand!" He brushed imaginary dirt from his lapels, perhaps convinced the battle in his head had taken place.

Arama's lips parted, and he followed Lara along the corridor. "Please, come back!" he protested. "I need to speak to you!"

Lara dipped her head and stared at the floor. She stomped from the restaurant, her high heels clicking against the tiles. A server approached her, and she waved him away, guilt prickling in her chest at having run out without settling her share of the bill. "He's paying." She waved her hand towards Arama, exacting her revenge in a passive aggressive protest. She promised herself she'd shove the cash through his letter box back in Market Harborough.

Arama's words chased her out into the frigid London night air. "No, Lara, please. I need to make this right!"

Paul caught Lara as she hailed a taxi. "What the hell was that about?" he demanded. Glancing around him at the busy street, he smoothed the bottom of his jacket over his hips and cringed at the stares. He tilted his head and pursed his lips. "Can we do our dirty washing in a less public setting?"

Lara groaned. "I was right the first time," she acknowledged, her tone sad. "You didn't care enough, Paul. I wish you well for the future."

She piled into the back seat of a black London cab, leaning her head back against the seat and closing her eyes.

"You okay?" the driver asked her, his cockney accent vibrant and jovial despite the late hour.

"I'm fine," she admitted. Her fingers fluttered over her heart and her shoulders relaxed. "I'm always fine."

Chapter Twelve

Back at the hotel, Lara retrieved the manuscripts from the safe in her room and spent the night comparing the copies to the originals. The cotton gloves made her hands hot with the central heating on, so she turned down the radiator. She knew every piece of binding, every neat stitch which held them together and every rigid, crusty, delicate page. Yellowing and tinged with the scent of decay provided a familiar, comforting blanket. Lara buried herself in history to absent herself from the pain of the present.

The first and third manuscripts contained regular entries relating to Queen Mary's persecution, although the damaged second artifact still hid its secrets. The museum's painstaking work promised to tease them free by degrees. "I just might have to read about it in a journal in a few years' time," Lara consoled herself out loud to the empty room.

'It is the third time this moon that the sacrament has been disturbed. There was warning previously but not on this occasion. The Queen's men flooded the town from the Leicester Road and overran it. They know we are still here and are determined to find us. Word from Rothwell is that our brothers are gone to the next life at the hands of the

soldiers. We held a mass in their honour, but the risk of discovery was great. The parishioners protect us and there are sentries posted at the four main routes into town but this time, the soldiers came through Rockingham Forest and caught us by surprise. We change nothing by hiding and yet we change nothing by dying. I fear we will all be eradicated for our faith.'

For such a short period, the records seemed concise and regular. Mary's zealous soldiers purged the countryside of protestants. She'd read of Henry VIII's ruthlessness against his perceived treacherous clergy, but the shortness of Mary's reign made Lara catch her breath with its ferocity. "You were your father's daughter," Lara mused. Though their opposite perspectives proved no less bloody.

'They say Smithfield stinks with the burning of clerical corpses. They do not even offer the dignity of slaying us first before they set the wooden faggots and our vestments aflame.'

Lara read through the night. The words held the familiarity of kisses from an old friend. But she read as an archivist, touching the parchment's physical form and imbibing the words and emotions which spawned them. Artifacts brought history to life. Her skill gave form to Hone's family relics. She knew him and could take him into the lives of others. When she closed her eyes, she saw his gnarled brown hands and toothless smile. She recalled the cheeky grin as she documented his upbringing and his tribal heritage. Her chest smarted with the memory of his ready tears as he spoke of the dead. He'd filled the dusty old trinkets with his lifeblood as they nestled in his age spotted hands, and commissioned Lara to keep them alive.

She dug into the essence of the priceless documents, searching for more than just history. Lara sought the men who created it, linking with them through their words. She brought their personalities and their terror into the present and offered them a voice for their outrage.

Their distress shook her to the core, their anguish piling on top of hers and burying her within its noxious folds. She relinquished her autonomy and allowed their sadness to suck her into their bottomless vortex.

Lara didn't use the sumptuous sheets or the fluffy pillows. She read all night, satiating herself with the misery of men willing to die for their faith. The injustice and political whims of leadership and monarchy cried out from the depths of history.

Flesh and blood possessed no value.

It never had and it never would.

The fourth manuscript documented some part of the English Civil war and Lara felt as though she stood in the midst of the chaos and bloodletting. As the central headquarters for the King's men, Market Harborough claimed an undisputed place in history with Naseby battlefield just up the road. But the priest hole, hidden and secret, became an unacknowledged hero in its own right, uncelebrated and until its discovery, unknown.

History revealed a custom for the third son of a noble family to enter the priesthood. The first son inherited the estate, the second joined the military, and the third entered the clergy. The third son of Lord Bowes of Northumberland entered the priesthood and acquired the living at St. Di's. When Cromwell nailed his colours to the mast and clashed with the King of England, the strong Bowes males followed him. With Harborough as the king's stronghold, it threw Edmund Bowes' safety into doubt. With his loyalties split, he worried about pastoring the town as his kinsmen attacked his flock. He spent many lonely nights in the priest hole, fearing discovery and death at the hands of his parishioners or the the king's men.

The scrawled bible verse in Latin called to Lara through the ages. A historian at Cambridge University translated it for her over email and it helped to soothe her pain.

'Job 19: 25-27 I know that my redeemer lives and that in the end he will stand on the earth. And after my skin has been destroyed, yet in my flesh I will see God; I myself will see him with my own eyes - I and not another."

Lara laid on the bed and stretched her limbs. She thought of the headstone she'd found in the graveyard in Little Bowden. The stone mason's words had faded over time but the name, Edmund Arthur Bowes remained. The central location of St Di's offered nowhere for the town's dead, instead relying on its sister church for burials. Age had ravaged the stone, lichen and moss encroaching on its weather pocked surface. Edmund Arthur Bowes died on the same day as Oliver Cromwell.

The growing town swamped the tiny graveyard as it grew. The headstones leaned at differing angles like rows of wonky teeth, bearing inscriptions that carried love and hope down the ages. '*Here lieth Edmund Arthur Bowes, Priest of this Parish. Fell asleep, 3rd September 1658.*'

Lara had cried at the graveside of a man she'd never met. The afternoon rain had weakened her arms as it drove its deluge against her umbrella. In the bedroom of the London hotel, she stroked the pages of research which showed the sad truth that Lord Bowes never claimed his son's body. He signed away their shared genetics, refused him entry to the family crypt and abandoned him to the town he'd served. His parishioners buried him with their own hands.

And he hadn't fallen asleep as his headstone declared. He'd been ripped apart by Cromwell's men and considered a traitor for assisting the king's wounded soldiers.

The futility of his death stung Lara with the overwhelming sense of waste. Man's inhumanity to man stretched down the ages. "I'm like you," she whispered. Her gloved fingers stroked the photocopy of Edmund Bowes' legacy. "I don't belong anywhere either."

As tears speckled her cheeks, Lara folded the extra copy of the secret manuscripts and separated them from the rest. She'd paid for from her own pocket, desperate to hold on to some part of the historical message. Her heart cried out to the spirits of the fallen priests. "I'll find somewhere beautiful, far away and create a monument to you all. You'll have the respect you deserve."

As she wiped her nose on hotel toilet roll and packed her small suitcase, Lara knew her time with the manuscripts was at an end. The task had provided the biggest challenge of her career, but only time would determine if she'd fulfilled the mandate.

Do no harm - The Archivist's Code. *Heal the legacy and move on.*

Lara told Paul she was going back to New Zealand on a whim. She'd wanted to keep him at arm's length, but as she sat in her first-floor room in the King Henry VIII hotel in London, the idea caught fire and became a reality.

The fretting ceased as Lara planned. She would return to the land of her forefathers. The wide green hills and feral mountains tugged at her blood and Hone's memory spoke to her from the grave. She'd go back and face her grief. *Carpe Diem. Seize the day*.

The artifacts needed to go home, and so did she. Instead of running away for once, she'd embrace life. She'd wring it out until it had nothing left to give.

Chapter Thirteen

"Lara please, wait, I can't stand this. Please talk to me?" His voice emerged with a begging edge he hadn't intended and the change of attitude stopped Lara slamming the door in Arama's face. She'd arrived home late from work. The relentless rain forced her to plod along the wet street in her sodden boots, water dripping off the end of her skirt. For the last two weeks Lara had avoided him and planned to continue the trend.

Arama emerged from his front gate at the same moment Lara negotiated hers and he dogged her steps up the path to her front door. Dressed in a white tee shirt and black shorts, he shivered against the freezing December rain. Lara almost made it inside before he spoke again. She sensed his intense brown eyes boring into the back of her head and intended to ignore him. Until she heard the catch in his voice. "Please, Lara. Let me put this right?"

She turned, her expression detached and impassive. Lara no longer got angry when she thought of Arama Hohaia-Livingstone. Not because she'd conquered her emotions, but because that part of her had died inside. Yet even in her emotionless state, she experienced shock at the sight of the man who stood in front of her. He looked dreadful. Dark circles rimmed his expressive brown eyes and even in the darkness, Lara saw how much weight had left his muscular frame. His clothes hung from him as though adorning a washing line and the numbness faded as she acknowledged regret for her part in his misery. It flickered as compassion and then died.

"Please can we talk?" he asked again. He lifted his arms out from his sides, his palms upwards. One of his shoelaces trailed in the puddle outside her door. Lara wondered if he'd watched out for her and mistimed his exit. But she couldn't ignore the look of hopelessness on his face. A sense of fear rose into her empty heart that if she didn't give him an opportunity to state his case, she'd regret it for the rest of her life.

Lara nodded and stood back to allow Arama to pass her. He bent down to take his trainers off in the hallway and looked lost, stood there in his socks with his dark, rain-soaked hair flopped over his eyes. Lara took off her boots and indicated he follow her down to the kitchen, where she uncorked a bottle of red wine. She almost made a jibe about *not being an alcoholic* but restrained herself, instead offering him a glass which he surprised her by accepting.

Arama sank down in one of the kitchen chairs and twirled the glass around on its stem. Neither of them spoke. Lara's heart pounded in her chest and it wrong-footed her until she traced the actual source of her discomfort. Knowing he was Hone's flesh and blood made her see him through different eyes. His little mannerisms and idiosyncrasies, previously unnerving were just achingly familiar. She saw his grandfather in every facet of him, raw and painful, yet healing. The generous old man smiled out at her from a grandson who never knew him. Arama never experienced his calm gentle wisdom, or sat on the top of a hill and watched the land roll out before him. The thought made Lara feel sad for what Arama missed, without even knowing it. "I wanted to explain," Arama began haltingly and shifted in his seat. His shorts rustled in the silence. "But now I'm here, I've realised I can't. I don't know what to say. I'm sorry, but that doesn't cut it. It's not good enough. *I'm* not good enough."

Lara gaped at him. She hadn't expected that. The scenarios she played out in her head so often only related to a man filled with arrogance and pride. They proved a waste of mental energy. Lara had no reply. She sank into a chair next to him at the table, the self-righteous wind sucked from her sails. Arama looked up at her through the folds of his fringe. He appeared broken. "Can you tell me about him? Please? My grandfather."

At first Lara didn't want to. She shook her head, not wanting to cheapen the memory of such a noble man by recounting his hopes and dreams to someone she believed didn't care. But the knowledge of Hone Hohaia wasn't hers to keep, and it burned on her tongue and in her heart, demanding to be told. The experience was cathartic for Lara, releasing some inner pressure which built up without her even knowing. "It was the best two years of my life," she heard herself declare. "I went out to New Zealand initially to do some extra university papers and link up with my father's heritage. Dad spoke with such love about his homeland. I looked for work before I left London, just on the off chance. There was this tiny advert in a newspaper, wanting someone to work part time to help restore a family legacy. It was so intriguing I couldn't ignore it and I rang Hone before I got on the plane. Without knowing me or taking up references, he offered to meet me at the airport and I accepted. I worried all the way there in case he turned out to be some kind of weirdo, or didn't turn up at all. But he was gorgeous. He held up this tiny little cardboard sign with my name spelt wrong on it and he stood with the taxi drivers and chauffeurs. I didn't know a single person in the entire continent and there was this little Māori man, greeting me at a few days' notice because he felt it was the right thing to do."

Lara smiled at the memory, her face endowed with an ethereal glow at the remembered ease of Hone's love for her. A stray tear plunged down her cheek and she brushed it away. "He talked to me on the way south and I agreed to work for him before we even reached Hamilton. That's what he was like, this honest champion of history. He reminded me of my father and I was content to stay with him for a while. His land was on the boundary of the Kaimai Ranges, at the foot of Mount Te Aroha and he had a granny flat which he let me live in. I travelled into the university in Hamilton two mornings a week to do my paper and Hone even lent me one of the farm vehicles to drive. I used to pick up shopping on the way back one day a week. The rest of the time we spent going through the *taonga*, the family treasures. He kept everything safe in a barn at the back of the property in a secure metal cabinet behind the tractors. We took things out one at a time, cleaned it and photographed it. I used a paper cataloguing system as that was all we had, but Hone would sit for hours and describe every piece. He felt he needed to do it."

Lara resisted the cruel sentence in her head, squashing it to prevent it leaving her mouth. '*For you,*' she wanted to say, '*we were doing it for you.*'

"My initial contract, informal as it was, lasted for a year. But we still hadn't finished by the December and Hone asked me to stay. I had nothing to come back to England for and I have New Zealand citizenship through my father, so I agreed. The day we finished cataloguing everything, Hone celebrated. We took the photograph of him standing next to the table of treasures and copied the family photograph from his living room wall. He got me to hand write a letter from him to you, telling you how desperate he was to meet you. It was never his choice to have you adopted. When his daughter died not long after you were born, the authorities took you away from him and he spent almost thirty years trying to find you. You have no idea how many private detectives ripped him off over the years. He found this one guy, Dan, who did everything he promised, and he tracked you down half-way through my second year with Hone."

Lara felt herself grind to a halt. The rest was too painful. Looking down, she seemed surprised to discover how wet the hands that writhed in her lap were. Her cheeks were sticky under her fingers.

"Why did *you* write the letter?" Arama asked, his voice hoarse.

"Hone was a farmer. His first language was Māori. He spoke English as well as anyone, but had no formal education. I wrote the letter to you because he couldn't. He dictated it to me. They're his own words."

"I never received it," Arama whispered. "Not until you brought it round to the house. I only ever met the detective. He turned up at my office and it was such a shock."

"Oh. Of course." Lara felt ashamed when she remembered her behaviour towards him. He seemed so arrogant and cruel. She wondered what it must have been like for him, receiving a plane ticket and an invitation to meet his grandfather, delivered without preamble by a private detective. It would have been catastrophic.

"Do you think it would have been different if you'd received all the photos and the letter? You know, before the detective turned up?"

Arama seemed to struggle. "I don't know," he replied. "I've thought about nothing else since I opened that envelope. What if I had seen all that first? What if I gave the matter more thought instead of throwing it all back in his face? I don't know, Lara. But I know I acted in haste and have the rest of my life to regret it."

"It devastated Hone," Lara said, trying to keep the sob from her voice. *Crushed* would have been a better word for it, because the old man seemed to shrink before her very eyes as the detective delivered the cruel and ungrateful return message after a long flight back from New York. Dan hadn't wanted to repeat it, but he'd discharged his duty with reluctance.

'It's too late. I don't need you.'

"The doctor said his heart gave out in the night, a week after Dan returned from America with your message.

The day before, Hone asked me to drive him into Hamilton and leave him outside his lawyer's office. He sent me off on an errand. I drove him home afterwards, and he went to bed and didn't wake up. I remember little of that period. A black cloud covers that time in my memory. Neighbours and old friends attended his *tangihanga*, but no family. He had nobody. I sat next to his body in the house for two days before they buried him, because no one came to relieve me. An elderly friend of his spoke for him on the *marae*. I couldn't even do that for him - I don't know enough Māori and women can't speak outside. I packed up and left the day after the funeral. He employed a farm manager who agreed to run everything as normal until the state came to claim the land and carve it into developments. You were his only heir."

Lara took a long sip of her wine and waited for the numbness to slide down her throat and into her heart. She had long since given up wiping away the stray tears. They became an unstoppable torrent of misery. *Better out than in.* "Hone didn't know you hadn't seen the envelope, Arama. And I assumed after your meeting with Dan, you'd sent it back unopened. It seemed possible that a mistake had it chasing you round the globe." Lara rubbed her face with both hands and sighed. "The day after the *tangi*, a stockman drove me to Auckland Airport and left me there. I rang Aunt Catharine in a state and she booked me a ticket online for the next flight home. Then she picked me up from the train station. She didn't even ask what happened. She just bailed me out, like always. All those hours of work were auctioned for the Crown. He wanted *you* to have it, not them."

Lara heard a strange sound and turned to Arama in confusion. It began as a sniff and progressed to a sob. His hand covered his face and his embarrassment caused him to writhe as he tried to get out of his chair. The wine glass tipped and crashed to the table, the red liquid spewing far and wide. Shock and dismay filled Lara's mind at the naked emotion leaking from his soul. She felt as wretched and cruel as if she'd turned the screws on a torture rack and stretched his body out thin and broken before her. "I'm sorry," she gasped, her voice high and breathy.

Arama seemed incapable of getting out of his seat. Without processing the irrational need to comfort him, Lara rose and wrapped her arms around his neck. She held him to her and crushed him as though trying to squeeze the pain out of them both.

Chapter Fourteen

In lonely desperation on the following Sunday, Lara walked to the church on Bath Street. Her confusing evening with Arama played on her mind. She hadn't seen or heard him next door since. Her soles kicked at loose gravel on the pavement as she walked, wishing she'd known what to do or say when he'd cried.

She'd stood over him and held him until her legs ached. Then he'd pulled her onto his knee and kissed her. They sat for an hour, holding each other like two drifting souls seeking clarity. Lara felt the surge of attraction again at the thought of his soft lips against hers and fought the rising emotion. Nothing would come of it, no matter how much she now acknowledged she wanted it to.

Arama's legs had wobbled as he rose and he'd thrust her away from him. Saying nothing, he strode from the house and slammed the front door behind him. Confusion and sadness swirled in his wake.

Lara's emotions veered through anger to sadness and back to desolation. The hum of white noise reverberated in her ears as she pushed the issue of her attraction on a loop in her head. Before bed, she'd touched the wall behind her head and imagined her soul connecting with

Arama's through the lath and plaster. Her soul sought a balm which wallpaper, and plaster couldn't administer.

Lara's wintry walk to the church comprised of a brisk, cold stomp through the streets. She headed in the direction she thought the building lay. Carried away with admiring the architecture of the houses on Newcombe Street, she almost forgot her destination. A man passed her, towing a reluctant puppy on a lead. Lara raised her hand to stop him, gratified by his open smile. "Is there a church around here?" she asked.

The puppy took the opportunity to sit on the pavement while the man gave her directions. By the time she arrived at the long, low church building, she heard the congregation singing, revealing a service already in full swing. Instead, she walked to a little play park up the road. "Coward!" she rebuked herself.

Two hours of looking like a child abductor and pushing random children on the swings made Lara even more morose. They recognised her from Kerry's art class and seemed keen to impress her with their death-defying feats on the play equipment. The teenage child-minders exhibited relief at her presence and bunched together, texting each other instead of talking.

"She works with dead people," a little girl commented. The teens slid their combined gaze towards Lara and then back to their phones.

After a while, they drifted away in their family groups to imbibe in sumptuous Sunday lunches. Lara found herself alone again. She strolled back the way she came, noticing the church car park was now empty apart from one car.

Feeling fairly safe and deciding to have it out with God in His car park if she couldn't do it in church, Lara wandered onto the property. It was Aunt Catharine's church, and she talked about it often. Lara remembered her aunt telling her how she met her business partner there about ten years ago. *Pity she didn't find a husband instead*, Lara griped. But Catharine was happy with her life. She was fiercely independent and by the time she breached the fifty-hurdle, had already decided she didn't want the complications.

Lara strolled towards the back of the property, where the car park dog-legged round behind the building. She remembered a discussion over email with Catharine where she'd mentioned helping to build a wooden cross. "Near a bench and by a grassed area," Lara murmured. Catherine and claimed she sometimes went there to think through a problem. Craving silence and space to collect her thoughts, Lara searched for the bench.

She found it where Catherine described and plonked down on the seat. Gazing around her, she sighed. "Why does my life suck when other people get away with murder?" she demanded of the empty car park.

A rough wooden cross stared back at her. Mounted on a wooden block, it appeared unsteady in the breeze which tugged at Lara's jacket. The corner of a notepad peeked from a drawer set in block. Curiosity nagged at Lara and she leaned forward and tugged at the wooden handle. Paper flapped on the pad as the breeze attacked the drawer's contents. She tried to hold it down one handed while rescuing a handful of ballpoint pens with the other. A laminated sign tacked to the front sheet of the pad encouraged her to write a list of her sins and hand them over to Jesus. Lara sat upright with a frown. "How does that happen then?" she demanded. "Does he turn up and just take them out of my hand?"

No one answered. The breeze whipped up the contents of the drawer and scattered tiny shreds of paper onto the grass. Lara dipped to ram the drawer shut before realising the papers contained fragments of handwriting.

Inquisitiveness made her chase a few of the ripped pieces and jigsaw them together again. Her eyes widened as she realised she held someone else's sins.

'Sorry God for letting my sister's hamster out.'

She cringed, recognising the confession of a child in the loopy script.

'Sorry for telling Daddy that I dint love him.'

Her eyes teared up at the hopelessness in the message. There seemed little worse than childish regrets.

'Sorry for breathing peenuts on my brother and setting off his peenut lurgy.'

"Oh," she breathed. "That's serious. I hope he survived." She compared the handwriting to the note confessing to letting the hamster out, but it appeared less stringy. Perhaps the church bred more than one miscreant. She put the bits of tatty paper back into the drawer and closed it, grabbing the pad and a pen. Then she sat back down. "Ok God," she said out loud. "Here goes nothing. I know you're there. I'm not sure why you keep trashing my relationships and killing the people I love. But I'll write my naughty stuff and then maybe you'll either fix it, or just leave me alone."

Lara wrote for twenty minutes and filled two of the sheets. It surprised her. "I never thought of myself a bad person," she mused. She included everything from as far back as she remembered and then pondered her crimes. "Now what?" she demanded. If she ripped up the paper and put it in the drawer, someone might read hers like she just read theirs.

Damn! She retrieved the pen from the drawer and added, '*92. Reading things that don't concern me,'* just underneath '*91. Stealing a brooch and an antique diary of national significance.'* She put the pen in her jacket pocket in case she needed to add anything else and then tutted. Everything she did created a problem for herself. She added number '*93. Stole pen from church.'* She figured it covered her in case she forgot to put it back before leaving.

A male throat cleared behind her, causing Lara to jump and swear. She contemplated getting the pen out again and adding number *94*. As the newcomer observed her, she wished she hadn't put numbers next to her sins and started counting.

"Rip it up and put it in the drawer," the man said, slumping onto the bench next to her.

"I don't want to," Lara replied. She stuck her chin in the air. "I might keep it, just to look at."

"Good idea," he answered, folding one of his legs over to rest on the knee of the other. "Maybe frame it and hang it in the toilet. I might copy that idea if you don't mind."

Lara shook her head. "Why should I mind? What are the odds on me *ever* going into your toilet?"

"You never know," he replied and smiled. Of average height and thin, he wore his hair cropped close his head. A pair of dark-framed, tinted glasses hid his eyes from her and a silver hoop earring dangled from one earlobe. A hole between the sole and the leather of his Doc Marten boot allowed a red sock to poke through the gap. "I'm the pastor here," he said with and Lara gulped. She hid her sheets of sins behind her back and closed her eyes. When she opened them again, he was still there, his blue eyes perceptive. She worried about how to get the pen from her pocket and into the drawer without looking like she intended to steal it. Number *93* had it covered, she reasoned.

"I think I might take my list home and burn it," Lara said, pleased with her brain wave. She wadded the pages up and tried to stuff them into her jacket. The pen kept getting in the way and poked them out again after administering a nasty stab to her hand. *Karma.*

"But the point of the exercise is to lay your sins at the foot of the cross," the pastor said.

"I'd rather burn them." Lara dug her heels in.

"That bad, hey?" A grin turned his lips up at the corners.

Lara glowered. "You have no idea."

The man relented and produced a cigarette lighter from his pocket. Lara's brow furrowed and curiosity budded at the thought of this holy man's sheet of sins. She wondered if covert smoking would be on the top line. *Probably not.* He had candles to light.

Lara reached out and grabbed the lighter with a muttered thanks. She had some trouble creating a flame in the gusting wind and almost gave up before a flickering amber glow wafted to life. The wind whipped up on purpose and made it hard to get the flame to stay against the paper but when it finally caught, it went for it like a bush fire. Fanned by the breeze, the flames licked up the sins towards Lara's hand at speed and she did the only thing she could. She dropped it.

It was just Lara's luck the paper missed the yards of grass and acres of car park and popped straight into the open drawer containing the pad and pen. The fire began cavorting with the drawer's contents. The pastor leaped the back of the bench and disappeared, leaving Lara to blow at the inferno in the wooden drawer. "Sorry Jesus!"

she wailed, faced with the prospect of the whole cross burning down in front of her face.

To her relief, the pastor reappeared with a fire extinguisher which gushed white foam into the drawer and left a residue on the foot of the cross.

As a precaution, he extracted the drawer and sprayed it again, just to be sure. His spraying appeared a little overenthusiastic as the fire died long before the drawer filled with foam. The wood inside looked charred and blackened and Lara waited for the pastor's shouts of anger and dismay. They didn't come. He turned to her with white foam on his glasses and giggled like a schoolboy. "Awesome," he said with a pyromaniac's glee in his eyes. "Ten years I've had a fire extinguisher in my office and never got to use it."

They sat on the bench together for an hour, intermittently snorting with laughter and chatting. Afterwards, Lara felt a lot better.

'94. Torched the cross. Found redemption.'

Chapter Fifteen

It was a few days before Christmas Eve. Arama had disappeared again and Kerry went with Lara to a local Christmas tree supplier on the edge of town. "Is our grumpy neighbour still being a pain?" Kerry asked as she struggled to put the back seats down in the Fiesta to fit the tree into the boot.

"No. And I should have got a smaller tree," Lara whinged. "It won't go in!"

"You're such a pessimist!" Kerry chided. She hauled her long coat and skirt beneath her elbows and climbed into the boot to battle with the tree. The rest of the sentence sounded muffled. Lara tilted her head to watch, seeing Kerry's bottom wiggling around in the small space.

"Hi Mrs Christmas." The shrill, sing-song voice held a trace of joviality. When Lara looked down, she saw the girl with the ponytails standing next to her. Thirty or more hair bobbles of varying colour erupted from her head in different directions and jaunty angles.

"Wow. Nice hair," Lara breathed. "How long did that take?"

"Ages." The child grinned up at her. "Good, isn't it?"

"Marvellous." Lara tilted her head again as Kerry grunted.

"What is Mrs Christmas doing?" The child cocked her head and squinted at Kerry's bottom.

"How do you know it's her?" Lara narrowed her eyes.

The child shrugged. "Just do." She affected a feckless wave in Kerry's direction. "We got a little tree." She skipped to a nearby vehicle. The tree draped over the side windows, secured on a roof rack with sturdy strops.

"Done it!" Kerry emerged backwards and grinned at Lara. "I tied it to the seat." She brushed needles from her hair and coat. "What's wrong?" she asked.

"How did ponytail-girl recognise you just from your butt?" Lara demanded.

"Dunno," Kerry replied. "You can't fool kids. Believe me, I've tried."

The same fun ensued at the other end of the journey. Lara parked the car with two wheels on the curb and the others on the double yellow lines on Nithsdale Avenue. Traffic built up behind them, unable to squeeze past with the parked cars lined up on the other side of the road. Having gone into the vehicle, the tree decided it didn't want to come out again.

"It won't budge!" Kerry wailed. "The plastic netting holding the branches down snapped. I bet that was the noise I heard as we went past Sainsbury's. It's stuck its branches out, and it's now wider than the gap."

In a true primary school style comedy, Kerry hung onto the trunk of the tree, kneeling half in and half out of the boot. Her backside went on display for most of Market Harborough to view. The tree exacted its revenge by shedding needles and bark all over the boot and the back of the rear seat. It still wouldn't release its hold on the vehicle.

Three local children from Kerry's class arrived to help, gripping her around the waist and hooking onto each other. Lara gripped the shoulders of the five-year-old at the back of the line. "Pull!" Kerry shouted, her voice muffled from inside the boot.

Everyone heaved but the last child let go of her sibling and Lara ended up on her backside on the wet pavement. "Oof!" she groaned. The five-year-old laughed, cushioned by her prone body. Lara pushed herself onto her knees, clutching her delicate ribs. "Oh, that hurts," she puffed.

"Stop messing about, Lara!" Kerry groaned, her face still in the boot. Tree branches obscured her view.

"Yeah!" said a little boy. "Stop messin' about, Lara!"

"Need a hand?" came a deep male voice and Lara took the proffered hand which hauled her to her feet Rubbing her jarred ribs, she looked up into Arama's face.

"Oh." The world stopped and the children's giggling faded. Lara swallowed. "No, we're fine, thank you."

"We are not fine!" Kerry snarled. "It won't come out."

"You don't look fine." Arama maintained eye contact with Lara. He reached up to snag a stray needle from her fringe. "Well, I didn't mean you." He cleared his throat. "You always look fine. I meant the thing in there." He flapped his hand towards the tree trunk protruding from the back of Catherine's car.

"Oh, great!" Kerry emerged from the boot backwards and rested her hands over her hips. She shook her head at Arama and Lara.

The little girls stared at the adults as though watching a cartoon. Bored, their brother stepped onto the bottom rung of Catherine's gate and rode it backwards and forwards. His eyes widened as the hinge gave and the gate slumped to the ground at an odd angle. He slunk back into place between his sisters, chewing his lip and practicing his most innocent expression.

The middle girl jumped up and down and clapped her hand over her mouth. “He wants to kiss her,” she hissed. Her sister turned to their brother. “Shut up,” she advised, anticipating his forthcoming complaint.

“But I’m cold,” he whined. He pursed his lips and clutched the front of his trousers. “I need a poo,” he said with a shudder. As one, the little family heaved a sigh and wandered back to their house two doors along from Arama’s.

Kerry shook her head in frustration and cleared her throat, hoping to get some attention. She’d ventured back into the boot and attempted to wrestle with the tree. A branch snaked behind her and whacked her bottom, blocking her exit. “I can’t get out!” she called. “Can someone help me? The bloody thing has me trapped. I swear it did it on purpose.”

A car horn honked as traffic built up behind the car. Ten sets of headlights cast highlights across her rounded bottom. A minibus squeezed between the side of the Fiesta and the line of parked cars on the other side of the road.

Arama swore and jumped to attention. He hauled the tree from the boot and manhandled it onto the pavement. Kerry released a series of screeches as it mashed her against the side window. He balanced the tree against the back of the car. “Key?” he snapped. He jerked his head towards Catherine’s front door.

“Sorry.” Lara’s fingers shook as she dug in her pocket and produced the key. She handed it to Arama and their skin touched.

He manhandled the tree through the front gate, swearing as it splayed its green branches against the doorframe.

Lara winced. "Mind the paintwork," she pleaded. Her shoulders slumped as Arama disappeared into the hallway, the tree scraping along the wallpaper.

"Great! He made that look easy. I'll move the car and you tell him where you want it," Kerry volunteered and Lara shook her head.

"No, I didn't want a tree. It was your idea. I'll move the car while you tell him where to put it. I need to get all this crap out of the back now."

"Let me move the car!" Kerry retorted, jumping into the driver's seat and starting the engine. Lara stood and watched the poor car bunny hop along the road, almost colliding with a lamppost as it cannoned off the curb. With a sigh, she entered the house and kicked off her shoes before shutting the front door behind her.

Arama cuddled the tree in the lounge, resembling a ballroom dancer about to begin a routine. Lara snorted before covering her mouth with her hand. He looked at her with a cocked eyebrow, his lips drawing into thin lines. Lara shrugged and pointed to the tree. "That's as far as I got," she admitted. "I don't know where to put it now."

"Do you have a bucket filled with soil?" he asked. He grunted and shifted the listing tree as it threatened to break free and crush him. His arms shook as though they ached. Lara shook her head. "Have you got some newspaper?"

Again the shake of the head. Arama looked around him. The tree shed needles in protest at the central heating. They scattered over his head and shoulders, spreading green spikes over the floorboards. "Do you have anything? Decorations, tinsel, any of that?"

"No. I don't want the tree."

With a cross shake of his head, Arama walked through the house, dropping green debris from one end to the other and the tree literally came in the front door and went straight out the back. Apart from being severed from its roots by a chainsaw, it got its wish.

Lara refused to let Arama's larger-than-life presence get the better of her. She smiled at the sense of peace which lit her heart on the bench with the hilarious pastor. It hadn't yet left her. She looked down at the scattered pine needles on the rug from her neighbour's hasty exit and reached for the contentment nestling inside. Her life was a mess, the pieces of her heart distributed about the earth like the needles, but it was her life and she now had the courage to live it. *Arama, or no Arama!*

He finished beating up the Christmas tree in the back yard and found Lara still in the lounge where he left her. She stood inside the doorway as though trying to decide something important. Kerry hadn't reappeared. Lara clicked her fingers. "The garage key is in the car. She might not see it." Guilt worried at her for not walking around in the dark and opening the garage door. "I should help her," she said to herself.

Lara turned to set off and ran into Arama's chest as he plucked up enough courage to stride into the room. "Ow!" she wailed as he stopped her going flying. *Again.*

"You need to stop doing that," he commented with an aggressive edge to his voice, born more of nerves than irritation. "Why don't you look where you're going?"

"*You* need to stop doing that!" Lara retorted, rubbing her side.

Arama exhaled and pushed Lara against the wall of the narrow hallway. He crushed her against him. "I can't keep doing this," he breathed, burying his face in her soft neck.

"Then don't," she whispered, her vibrant blue eyes glittering with mischief and stubbornness. Arama's breath came in short huffs as he placed his lips near Lara's. The sexual tension between them arced and hissed in the small space, covering them both with a hot, tingling sensation. Arama's eyes were full of challenge and fear as Lara relaxed and leaned back against the wall for support. She smiled, resigned to the inevitable attraction.

Like an explosion, Arama scooped his arm around her back and Lara felt the tension leave as he kissed her neck, her cheeks and lips. For someone who said he couldn't keep doing this, Arama seemed to manage fine and Lara struggled to come up for air underneath the man's latent passion. "What is this?" Lara whispered, creating soft wisps of breath against Arama's fringe.

He gazed at her, one corner of his lips rising in a tiny smirk. "We both know what this is," he replied, lifting her up around the waist so he could kiss her at his own height. Lara put her arms around his neck and kissed the end of his nose, wrapping her legs around his thighs.

"I knew it!" Kerry's victorious voice erupted from the kitchen doorway behind them. "Now I'm glad I stayed outside in the dark and cold, cleaning *your* car with that rubbish hoover thing!"

Lara clapped her hand over her mouth in and turned away to hide her embarrassment. She felt like a teenager caught necking with the neighbour in her aunt's hallway. Arama huffed with irritation at Kerry's interruption.

Nobody could move in the tiny space even if they wanted to. Kerry blocked the kitchen doorway, and the other two grid locked the hall. "How about I stay in here then?" Kerry humphed and turned away, opening and slamming cupboards in the kitchen. Glasses clinked, and a cork popped. Lara remained frozen against the wall, eclipsed by Arama, who held onto her, chewing his bottom lip and saying nothing. Dread snaked around Lara's heart again. *Don't be silly. You're leaving.* Her mind rebuked her in measured tones.

Arama's tasteful tie was askew on his neck from the fight with the tree and pine needles decorated his expensive dark pinstriped suit like pointy confetti. A pulse beat in his neck from the strain of holding Lara up and her eyes strayed to the muscle bulging through a small gap between the buttons of his shirt. The sound of wine glugging into three glasses rent the air, making Lara want to snigger, but still neither of them moved or said anything.

Arama let Lara's body slide down his, the wallpaper behind her making small sounds of objection as her clothes rubbed against the weave. He pulled Lara's hand away from her mouth with a gentle action, turned it over palm up and kissed her fingers. His handsome face twitched with uncertainty, but he risked it again and leaned forward to kiss Lara's full lips, this time putting more meaning into it than lust. He groaned as Lara responded, hungry for contact with him as she found the balm for her aching heart. Arama was just getting into his stride when the front door flew open, banging against the wall behind it with a mighty crack. The formidable figure of Aunt Catharine stood framed in the doorway, back lit by the streetlamps and the darkness outside.

Arama jumped and looked guilty, Lara looked distressed, Aunt Catherine looked horrified and Kerry's face expression held nothing of use. "Mmnn," she said, her voice sounding tinny with her face stuck in a wine glass in the kitchen. She shivered with pleasure as she swigged a very expensive merlot hidden at the back of the cupboard.

Catharine's face settled into a satisfied smirk. She pointed an accusing index finger at Arama. "That's not quite what I meant when I asked you to look out for my niece," she said.

Arama raised his chin higher in defiance, one hand clasped round Lara's waist and the other beneath her chin. Lara pulled away from him, her cheeks reddening to the hue of a tomato.

"Why is the gate hanging off its hinges and where has all this foliage come from?" Catharine demanded, glaring at the needle strewn hallway.

She wheeled her case into the hallway. "Fine! Nobody answer me. I'll just take my gear into the lounge then, shall I?" As she stepped away from the doorway, her companion entered behind her.

Arama and Lara reacted in different ways.

Arama jumped as though shot and took a step backwards. But Lara gave a whoop of joy and ran to the man in the doorway, leaping clean off the floor and ending up in his arms. "Hello, *kōtiro!*" the visitor laughed as he swung her round in the tiny space and kissed her forehead.

Chapter Sixteen

Catharine refused to let Arama run away. "Don't you dare, young man!" She detained him with all kinds of whispered threats and he sat in a corner of the lounge, his grumpy self restored. Kerry opened another bottle of wine and fetched two more glasses but stashed the lovely bottle of red down the side of her armchair and helped herself when nobody was looking. Lara sat on the sofa cuddled up to the private detective and looked happier than she had for ages.

Dan was in his early sixties, tall, dark haired and fluent in Te Reo Māori. He served as a cop, but retired after a nasty shooting in Auckland left him unfit for active duty. He set up his detective agency and became friends with Hone and Lara in the old man's quest to find Arama Hohaia-Livingstone. His first meeting in New York with the angry young man proved an unpleasant one. Arama glared at him from across the room.

"I came to see you after the *tangihanga,*" Dan said, turning to Lara. His lyrical tones washed over her with comfort and familiarity. "The station hands said you'd already gone. Why would you run like that? Silly girl." He wrapped her delicate hand in his strong paw and looked on her with compassion. "The lawyers went frantic," he told her. He frowned as her eyes widened and she held her breath.

"Oh, that," she replied. Her colour drained away, leaving her back where she began two months earlier. Catharine stared at her with concern in her blue irises.

Dan had two commissions. The first involved finding Hone's heir and informing him of his grandfather's death. The second role meant tracking down his replacement. Both jobs required a face-to-face consultation.

Dan made the arduous journey back to New York, relishing the chance to tell the jumped-up executive he would no longer inherit. He hadn't thought beyond that moment but trusted something would come to him once the conversation began. "I went to see him," Dan jabbed his finger in Arama's direction. "But I arrived too late. He'd gone." Exhaustion filtered over Dan's expression and he relived the moment of defeat. "I sat with my head in his hands, jetlagged and exhausted, not knowing where to go from there. The receptionist bought me coffee and introduced me to Mr Livingstone's business partner."

"Yes, Dan's tale intrigued me," Catharine interrupted. "As the story unfolded and Lara's name featured, things clicked into place for me. I knew they were keeping things from me!" She slapped her thigh and glared at Lara's keepers. "Kerry's been vague and Arama, deliberately evasive. So, 'Come on!' I told poor Dan. 'I'm going home and you're coming with me.'"

Dan put his arm around Lara's delicate frame, offering the fatherly affection he'd planned to give her after Hone's funeral. Lara denied him the chance with her hasty exit. "The day before Hone Hohaia died, he met with his lawyer in Hamilton and revoked his former will. You're no longer his heir," Dan informed Arama with obvious satisfaction, jabbing a finger at Arama's rigid body.

The ex-police officer called Hone his friend, and the task gave him great pleasure. His tired face relaxed into a smirk at the dispossessed man in the overstuffed armchair. Dan turned to face Lara and took her chin into his hand. She was beautiful, perfect. He smiled at her, mistaking Arama's obvious anguish for the loss of his fortune and not possessiveness over Lara.

"Hone left everything to you, Lara," Dan said. "The farm, the livestock, everything. And he dictated this letter to the lawyer." He handed her a sealed envelope and everyone in the room held their breath. Everyone except Kerry. She slumped in her chair as the room spun and the faces of her class zoomed around above her head. Swatting at them caused them to dissipate like fog. She produced the bottle from the side of her chair and topped up her glass. Catharine's eyes narrowed to disbelieving slits as she tapped her fingers on the arm of her chair in fury.

Lara fingered the crumpled envelope in her fingers, her face unreadable. Catharine watched with concern as Arama stood up in a jerky movement and left. She had worked with him for ten years and known him for longer. He presented like an open book to her. In his expression she read hurt, dismay, a strange mix of fear and then a perplexing hint of *relief*.

While Lara went upstairs to her room and pushed the envelope around on the bedspread without opening it, Catharine drove into town to fetch some food. The Christmas tree leaned up against the wall outside the back door jumped on her as she passed. She screamed and battled her way from beneath the spiky needles. Kerry shuffled behind her like a drunk, sniggered and farted at the same time, whooping with exhilaration at her cleverness. "Oh, you're a worry!" Catharine sighed and steered the silly girl towards the garage, where Kerry lay the passenger seat down flat and went to sleep. She snored while Catherine waited to pick up the chips.

Arama lay on his bed; his arm stretched backwards so his fingers rested on the wall behind him. He heard Lara breaking her heart for a man he never knew and ached, both for himself and her.

It was the memory of Hone which made Lara cry; his gentle trusting face and the way he made nobodies feel like somebodies, with only a smile or word. Lara closed her eyes and conjured up his face and voice. But when she opened the envelope, he was there with her in person, his soft lyrical tone calling out to her from the *urupa*, the burial ground of his ancestors.

'Tamāhine, my daughter. I trusted when I placed the advert for an archivist that it would fulfil all my dreams. You didn't disappoint me. But I didn't understand the true nature of my dreams. What we achieved satisfied a deep desire for acceptance. That is what you gave to me.

The damage done to my poor mokopuna proved too great to allow him to forgive, and that grieves my soul. Only you will understand how much. You, who endured my aimless ramblings for two glorious years, allowing an old man to voice his battered memories and give them value. Your presence brought me healing kōtiro, more than you will ever know. I am at peace with my decision. I am the last of the Hohaias. There is no-one to hand my mana onto. The tangata whenua demand the safekeeping of our property. I place it into your capable care. My Arie is out there and curiosity will drive him home. I believe in my heart it will all work out somehow. Guard the whenua with your life until the time is right. You will know when that is.

Your ever loving friend,

Hone Wiremu Tane Hohaia.'

Hone called her 'daughter,' *tamāhine*. Lara cried as though unravelled from the inside, understanding afresh what life had ripped away from her. Again. He had entrusted the *whenua*, the land to her. It bestowed on her a tremendous honour and a terrible responsibility.

Lara blew her nose and wiped the tears away with her sleeve. Something changed within her and she sensed herself detaching from the little sleepy town, the rambling English ancients and the spectre of her dead parents. Her heart-lines switched allegiance to the land of her paternal forefathers. She would find her father's *whanau* and dig her own family trenches deep, burying her father's roots so no one would ever loosen them.

A new lightness of spirit consumed Lara as she found her place in the world and the God of Heaven smiled as the wind continued to sweep at the charred remnants of a scrawled *'91. Stealing a brooch and an old dairy.'*

Chapter Seventeen

Arama opened the front door in a tee shirt and jeans. Even dressed casually, his clothing overlaid his sculpted muscles with precision. He appeared wide awake and refreshed. His damp hair revealed he'd just come from the shower. Lara knew that anyway. She'd watched him go for a run and return home. She waited for the water to stop running next door before descending to the street and knocking on his door. "Am I disturbing you?" she asked. He winced, standing back from the door to invite her inside without speaking.

His lounge lay to the left and Lara followed him, finding a mirror image of Catharine's house. Arama's furnishings were black and chrome, a masculine bachelor pad for the free and single. "Drink?" he offered, peering out from beneath his fringe. Lara nodded, for want of anything else to say. She followed him down the hallway into the kitchen and put the contents of her full hands on the glass dining table.

Remembering her manners, she took her shoes off and then looked in distaste at her feet through the glass, noticing the hole in the toe of her right sock. Arama brought two mugs of steaming coffee to the table. He hadn't asked her what she wanted. "What's all that?" he asked, looking at the cotton bag nestled next to the plastic carrier. His sideways glances showed he sensed it held the real reason for Lara's visit. Lara smiled and pushed the carrier bag towards him with a smile.

Arama put his hand inside and drew out the three bars of New Zealand chocolate. A small smile played on his lips. "Kiwifruit, feijoa and possum?" Lara nodded and Arama smirked. "Well, I've missed the first two but I'm not sure about the last one," he said, fingering the odd ridges in the packet.

"It's not a real possum," Lara said, trying to be helpful. "It's hokey pokey and caramel. They brought it out as a joke..." She bit her lip. "Sorry about the lumps in it. I should have brought it round that first day you arrived home. It melted upstairs, and it's lived in the fridge ever since."

It all seemed so long ago and academic. Arama chewed his lip. "Lara are you married?" he blurted and looked as though the question had burned a hole in his soul for far too long.

"No!" she bit, amazed, distracted from her purpose in visiting him. "Why on earth would you think that?"

Arama banged the heel of his hand on his forehead but kept his eyes closed. "Kerry said something on the way back from the hospital that day. She said you didn't want me to know you were something beginning with 'm' and then she stopped and wouldn't tell me what she meant."

"*Māori!*" Lara exclaimed. "I didn't want you to know I had Māori heritage. I suspected you had connections back in New Zealand, and I didn't want you to unpick my reasons for leaving."

"Why not?" Arama's question was almost a shout of frustration and it made Lara jump.

Why indeed? "That brings me to what's in here," she began. "You see, I had this theory that if I told you what I'd done, it could get me into a lot of trouble. It's the two degrees of separation theory. Everyone in New Zealand is related to or knows someone you know. It sounds ridiculous, but it's true."

Arama shook his head and raised his hands, palms upwards. "Why are you telling me this?" He shook his head as though to help him process her words.

"Ok," Lara tried again. "When Hone died, and no one could locate you, I thought the state planned to claim his assets. So, I stole some items including the brooch he gave his wife on their wedding day. It came from his mother and the generation before hers. I couldn't bear to watch it auctioned off and end up as another relic in a museum. It has a tale all of its own to tell. It came to your family through '*utu,*' a process of righting the wrongs. Your ancestors raided another tribe after they killed one of Hone's female ancestors. The injured party took valuables as reparation..."

"I know what *utu* is," Arama whispered.

"Of course, you do." Lara's nerve left her. She struggled to continue. "I also brought a manuscript with me. It was a diary compiled by Hone's mother and the women of the family before her. Your great grandmother documented your birth and other events from that time. Hone's wife died not long after your mother. The other women didn't survive." She tapped the front of the diary. "This inscription shows the paper is a gift to the family in the early 1800s. A local missionary records spending time with them in his own memoirs. I can give you his details when you're ready. They made the paper from delicate calf-skin, bound into the kauri frame at a later date. Wood pulp paper from that time hasn't survived as well as this." Lara realised nervousness made her babble as she awaited his condemnation for her theft. She morphed into 'Lara the historian' and feared she'd bored him. She ploughed on. "Several generations of your female *whanau* documented their history. Their stories got passed down the generations of women and they continued it. They drew pictures and created patterns at first. Later, though some of the writing is hard to read, your grandfather and I translated it for you."

Lara pushed the cloth bag towards Arama's shaking fingers. He seemed too afraid to touch it. Anguish back lit his eyes as he appealed for her to take it away from him. "I know, Arama," she whispered, touching his hand with her fingers. "I know your mother was only fifteen and I know your father raped her."

"It's why nobody wanted me." Lara had to lean forward to hear him. "*She* didn't want me. Nobody did. As soon as the foster parents found out, they sent me back to the children's home. Over and over again."

"It's not that she didn't want you!" Lara cried in horror. "She died a month after you were born. She suffered untreated complications and died. Hone tried to keep you, but there were no women left to help him. The authorities took you away, and he lost track of you. He didn't *want* that!"

Arama's expression was raw and open; everything laid bare for Lara to see. It was agony to look at. She stroked his fingers and took a deep breath. "Arama, these things are yours, not mine. It's ironic that I believed I'd stolen something that he'd given to me. But I think it's important for you to read them, even if you can't bear to keep them. Look," Lara found the next part difficult. "I believe Hone wanted me to act as a custodian. For you. For your legacy. I don't think he meant me to keep your heritage, just look after it for you. Until you're ready."

Arama shook his head with instant objection but Lara intended to finish her mission. "Read the letter he wrote to me," she whispered, pulling Hone's heartfelt words from her pocket and placing the thin paper on the table. Creased and worn from constant re-reading, the type showed through from the back of the paper. "Read it, but please give it back before I leave. It's all I have left of him which belongs only to me."

Lara bit her lip and suppressed her own tears. The handsome man in front of her with his head hanging low, appeared dismantled. He needed time to put himself back together again, without an audience.

Chapter Eighteen

Christmas Day arrived. Lara did some last-minute shopping to account for all the extra guests residing at the house on Nithsdale Avenue. Catherine invited Dan to stay in the attic room and ensconced herself back in her luxurious back bedroom. Arama made no attempt to engage with Lara, the silence behind her headboard eerie. She left him alone to deal with his hurts.

Catharine and Dan rescued the tree from outside the back door and decorated it together. Too much red wine and hilarity created a gaudy affair with strings of tinsel and mismatched baubles. But the cat seemed happiest of all; his equilibrium restored. Kerry planned to spend Christmas day with her new man and his family but loved the present Lara gave her. "Oh my gosh, I love them!" She squealed with enthusiasm at the souvenir from Lara's trip to London. The beautiful Harrods earrings sparkled from her lobes as Lara watched her get into her boyfriend's car.

Lara sat in the lounge with a novel in her hands, lost in thought as the flames flickered in the hearth in front of her. Noise in the hallway signalled an arrival, but Lara assumed it was just Dan coming home after his run. He promised to be back for lunch. She heard voices and the lounge door opened to admit Arama. Nothing seemed to hold any fear for Lara anymore and she greeted Hone's grandson with a friendly smile and a wave. He'd dressed in neat shirt and slacks, but his darting eyes betrayed his nervousness. "Hi," he said, his voice catching in his throat.

"Sit your bum down, man!" Catharine reappeared and pressed a glass of mulled wine into his shaking hand. Arama looked around for somewhere to put it. He settled it on the mantelpiece and then came to sit on the ottoman in front of Lara as soon as Catharine left the room. Lara moved her feet aside for him, but he reached for the nearest ankle with one giant hand and held on, seeming to need physical contact.

"I read the letter," he murmured. "I read it all, the diary as well. It proved cathartic." He reached inside his back pocket and took out the notepaper, placing it with care on the arm of the chair. Lara looked at it but made no move to scoop it up, despite her fingers twitching. She missed having Hone's words to comfort her. "Thanks for all the work you did to translate the diary. I wouldn't have been able to read it otherwise. I know little *Te Reo*."

Lara nodded and avoided adding that Hone translated it. She had only written his words down. And it was the old Māori, not the more recent, anglicised version.

Arama stood up and retrieved his glass. His hand shook as he sipped from it too fast, causing himself to splutter. "Catharine asked me to lunch. Is that ok with you?" He didn't turn to look at her when he asked his question, perhaps afraid of her reaction. His back looked stiff and poised for a swift exit.

"Of course, it is," Lara replied, wishing he would just turn around and face her. He was gorgeous, and she never grew tired of his dark features. He kept his back to her and reached into his pocket, saying nothing as he dug around for a moment. His broad back showed through his pale blue shirt, the muscle definition stretching the fabric. Lara felt a jolt of desire begin in her stomach and beat it down again. She'd already booked and paid for her flight from Birmingham Airport. Sadness crawled through her veins as her heart recognised a missed opportunity with this beautiful man. It gnawed at her insides, not as easily beaten as the other emotions which had consumed her in the last six months.

Lara's fingers strayed to the scruffy paper, sensing Hone's presence in the words hidden inside, his own scrawled signature at the bottom of a line of neat typing. It's where he must have gone that day when she drove him to town. She imagined him waiting around for the secretary to type it, so he could sign it and lodge it there. He didn't need to sign anything - it wasn't a legal document. But he'd wanted her to see his mark and understand the significance.

"Thing is," Arama struggled. For a capable professional, he was certainly making a meal of whatever he was trying to say. Catharine waited outside the door listening to every word. "Bloody hell man, will you just get on with it!" she sighed.

"Seeing as you're not married, and I got that misinformation wrapped round my neck," Arama turned, his face a picture of terror. "It was the only thing that stopped me asking you out. Apart from the fact you seemed to hate me. I didn't help matters by behaving like an idiot, but there's this ridiculous attraction between us." Arama stopped mid-flow, knowing he'd made a mess of everything. Confusion and curiosity masked Lara's expression. "I believe in soul mates and I know you're mine. I wish we'd got off to a better start, and that you weren't leaving so soon." He dropped to one knee in front of Lara and presented the little maroon velvet box. His fingers shook. "This seems like the stupidest thing I've ever done, but I can't let you go without asking. We've only known each other a few months, and I didn't make you like me much." The box tumbled out of his fingers onto the floor and he swore at himself.

Outside in the hallway Catharine clamped her hand over her mouth to stop herself screaming in frustration. Arama retrieved the box and held it up to Lara. He looked like a child presenting his best drawing, vulnerable and open. She took it from him in gentle fingers, not quite understanding his intent. "I don't want the land," Arama stuttered, "and I'm not trying to stop you leaving. But I have to say this, otherwise I'll die not knowing if we...if it..." He took a massive breath which almost choked him. "Will you marry me?"

Lara gasped as Catharine burst through the door, her arms open wide. "Congratulations. Of course, she bloody will!"

Epilogue

The tiny boy's slender brown frame tumbled down the grassy hill, tossing his body head over heels again and again. He loved it. His giggles drifted across the landscape.

"Tane Hohaia, get back here now!" his mother shouted. "And for goodness' sake, put some clothes on!"

"No fanks," he called back as he finished tumbling. "This tickles. I like it."

Lara sighed and chased the four-year-old down the hill. Running seemed ill advised at this late stage of her pregnancy. Arama's son rolled around in the grass, completely free as his little shorts and tee shirt flapped in his mother's hands. A law unto himself, he exuded a sense of freedom incomprehensible to both his parents. His affinity to the whenua seemed ethereal. Lara smothered a smirk at his antics as the long grass enfolded him in its willing grasp and the pollen dotted his black hair with kisses. It's why they'd come home. For this.

In her head she heard Hone's deep laugh, sensing a dying man's intention. He promised it would all sort itself out, and it had. She glanced down at the brooch on her cardigan, way too opulent for the clothes it clung to. The delicate white bone glinted in the sunshine of a New

Zealand summer's day and the precious jade inlay winked at her. It was Arama's gift to her on their wedding day, his grandmother's brooch, stolen, returned and now given.

The little boy in the paddock below kissed the ground and hugged it. He sensed the contentment of the land beneath his tiny hands and the satisfaction of the tangata whenua, his heritage - the indigenous people of the land who bound him to them by his birthright. "Can we see it again?" the child yelled from the deep paddock and Lara sighed.

"Ok, but only if you hurry."

The child hauled himself up and ran to his mother, reaching out for her hand. Dirt streaked his naked body, and he displayed no shame. His beautiful spirit made Lara smile with his enthusiasm for life. At the top of the hill stood a monument made from local stone and engraved by a stone mason. "Who is them peoples?" Tane asked, just like he always did.

"Priests," Lara replied, running her finger down the grooves in the hard, grey stone. "Men who died for their faith. They hid in gaps in churches called priest holes from evil men who wanted to kill them. When they died, nobody remembered their names or cared."

"But you cared, didn't you, Mummy?" the boy said, his dark eyes searching her face. Lara nodded.

"Yes, I cared. I made them a promise and I've kept it."

"That's nice, Mummy." Tane observed the grey stone and the list of names and dates carved into it. He'd watched the big crane slide it into place and observed his mother's serious face as it bonded itself to the hill. She held a bunch of papers in metal tongs and his serious father lit them and watched them burn, the blackened pieces scattering on the wind and carrying them to other places.

Tane broke free from Lara's grasp and danced with excitement, performing his own haka for her benefit, little feet stamping the ground and tiny fists beating his proud breast as he chanted and postured. Lara watched him with pride as he finished and she resisted the urge to clap.

"Who is that name?" Tane climbed onto the stone step and pointed to the inscription near the bottom.

Lara smiled at her son. *"Edmund Arthur Bowes. Killed in Market Harborough town centre, England, September 3rd 1658."*

"Where is...Market...Har...Harborough?" The child beamed, pleased at getting the complicated word out and enjoying the sounds rolling from his tongue.

"It's where I found Daddy," Lara said, turning away from the monument.

"Was he lost there?" the child persisted, showing signs of growing bored with the conversation.

"We both were," Lara stared at her son as a familiar feeling began in the pit of her stomach.

"What does my name mean again?" Tane shouted back over his shoulder, already rolling over and over in the long grass. He knew. But he wanted to hear her say it out loud, there, in that place so the tangata could hear.

"Tane means 'man,'" Lara called, feeling the familiar tug at the base of her spin encircling her stomach and filling her with relief. "About time, baby," she spoke to her unborn infant, already two weeks overdue.

"What, Mummy?" the little boy called. "What you saying?"

"Hohaia is Josiah in Māori," she called back, trying to keep the pain out of her voice. "Please come on Tane. I need to get back to the house and call Daddy."

"Yey, Daddy!" The reaction was instant. At the thought of his capable father, the little boy bounced up straight away and traversed the hill buck naked. He set off towards the house nestled into the foothills of Mount Te Aroha, his mother following more slowly behind. Lara paused every few minutes to brace herself against a contraction.

Thousands of miles away the harsh English winter battered Market Harborough, grid locking roads and railways. But the sundial on the side of St. Dionysius Church spire tried to record the hour despite no sun to create the needle's shadow. The moonlight glinting off its polished surface gave away the location of the secret priest hole, not that many knew of its existence still. It provided a silent beacon that nobody understood.

Around the metal prongs of the dial, ensconced in the cloudy darkness of night, the Roman numerals displayed the time. But on the uppermost side above it, an inscription carried a vital missive to all who cared to look up. It called out its urgent message during daylight hours for the benefit of passing locals or visiting strangers. Its twin echoed back from a green paddock in New Zealand, the heavy stone weathering under the same cruel sun. It sent a coded communication from wise ancestors to a busy world which grew deaf and blind in humanity's complicit danger.

'Improve The Time' it cried.

But nobody listened. Not then and not now.

A note from the Author

I thoroughly enjoyed writing this novel. I lived in Market Harborough for almost six years, raising four small children in the folds of its rich tapestry. It was not an easy time in my life but I was welcomed there. My characters are always a smorgasbord of many people whom I either know or imagine, but I am sure that very occasionally, my good friends will see themselves reflected in Lara's complicated friendships.

I am certain that local historians will be scandalised at my abuse of the town's colourful history and I apologise for any frustration or anger at my apparent ludicrous artistic licence. I am an archivist by trade and a romantic at heart. And the honest truth is that I love Market Harborough and whilst I have mangled its legacy, mean it no ill will.

I have been upstairs in the Old Grammar School, celebrated Christmas Eve in St. Di's, walked home down Nithsdale Avenue and spent many happy hours at the primary school and the church on Bath Street, all of which feature in this novel. It's a beautiful town.

If even one person reads this novel and decides to visit, maybe walks around the town, admires the Old Grammar School and buys a coffee then what more can I ask?

For Market Harborough, whilst I am thousands of miles away, I have sent a friend to see you in my place.

Kind regards,

K T Bowes

Dear Reader,

I would love it if you could leave a review at your usual retailer.

I find the opinions of readers helpful and constructive. Reviews are the Holy Grail to an author as they cause our work to sink or swim. It is the bench mark for other readers and can determine whether our work will be successful and reach many or none. It doesn't have to be an essay or a literary criticism. A few words about what you liked would be most appreciated. The shortest review I ever received for my work was, 'Great,' accompanied by five stars and the longest was a whole video from a gorgeous woman in the USA. My favourite to date has to be the lady who said, 'I read until my eyes fell out.' I keep looking at that one because it makes me laugh.

You can review on my website, ktbowes.com. Go to the book's buy page where you can follow through to your own retailer and leave a review for me.

And hey, let me know when you've done it. I'd love to hear from you.

Say Hello

You can find the author hanging out on social media in the following places.

Check in and say hello. Maybe suggest she gets back to writing and stops watching cat videos.

FACEBOOK
https://www.facebook.com/NZauthorKTBowes/

INSTAGRAM
https://www.instagram.com/k_t_bowes

Copyright Notice

Other Books by this Author

The Hana Du Rose Mysteries Series:

Logan Du Rose

About Hana

Hana Du Rose

Du Rose Legacy

The New Du Rose Matriarch

One Heartbeat

The Du Rose Prophecy

Du Rose Sons

Du Rose Family Ties

Du Rose Vendetta

Phoenix Du Rose

****

The Calculated Risk Series:

The Actuary

The Actuary's Wife

The Actuary in Trouble

The Heart of The Actuary

****

Troubled series for teens:

Free from the Tracks

Sophia's Dilemma

A Trail of Lies

Gone Phishing

****

New Zealand Soccer Referee Series:

All Saints

****

Escaping the Back Country NZ Series:

Pirongia's Secret

Deleilah

****

UK based mystery/romances:

Artifact

Demons on Her Shoulder

****

Humorous Cozy Mystery Series from New Zealand

Dead Straight

Bad Hair Day

Side Parting

ontent.com/pod-product-compliance
Group UK Ltd.
Keynes, MK11 3LW, UK
0726
00018B/137